Murder in Shangrila

Murder in Shangrila

A Small Town Murder Mystery

By

LOUISE A. MARASSO

MURDER IN SHANGRILA
A SMALL TOWN MURDER MYSTERY

iUniverse books may be ordered through booksellers or by contacting:

iUniverse
1663 Liberty Drive
Bloomington, IN 47403
www.iuniverse.com
1-800-Authors (1-800-288-4677)

Because of the dynamic nature of the Internet, any web addresses or links contained in this book may have changed since publication and may no longer be valid. The views expressed in this work are solely those of the author and do not necessarily reflect the views of the publisher, and the publisher hereby disclaims any responsibility for them.

Any people depicted in stock imagery provided by Thinkstock are models, and such images are being used for illustrative purposes only.
Certain stock imagery © Thinkstock.

ISBN: 978-1-4917-8236-1 (sc)
ISBN: 978-1-4917-8235-4 (e)

Library of Congress Control Number: 2015919140

Print information available on the last page.

iUniverse rev. date: 12/10/2015

Inhabitants of Elden in order mentioned:

- Jake, a Handyman
- Mathew Reardon, Sgt. with the Elden Police Force
- Kevin Branch, Detective with the Elden Police Force
- Elena Vitki, a former resident of Elden
- Frederik Vitki, Elena's brother, also a former resident of Elden
- Karl Jenkins, Owner of the local Laundry & Mending Company and Elden Postmaster
- Vincent Delaney, a neighbor of Karl Jenkins
- Ted, Elden Mail Carrier and part-time Shangrila employee
- Sharon Retton, Swimming & Yoga instructor at Shangrila
- Rodney Kastor, Elden Sheriff and Town Constable
- Henry Jordan, a local handyman
- Mr. & Mrs. Chandra, Proprietors of the 7-Eleven Store near Elden
- Mr. Sharma, Proprietor of the Mechanics Shop adjacent to the 7-Eleven Store
- Justin Haber, a student just turned 16
- Alden Haber, Father of Justin
- Gloria Retton, Mother of Sharon Retton and wife of Bill Retton
- Bill Retton, Husband of Gloria and Bank Manager in Hemmings
- Cecily Watson, Girlfriend of Justin
- Nelam Chandra, Niece of Mr. & Mrs. Chandra, visiting from India
- Dora, Owner of Dora's Café in Elden
- Dr. Gregory, Physician and head of Elden Clinic
- Bob, Moving Van driver
- (Mr. & Mrs.) Frank Grayson, Manager of Tecto Associates in Victor

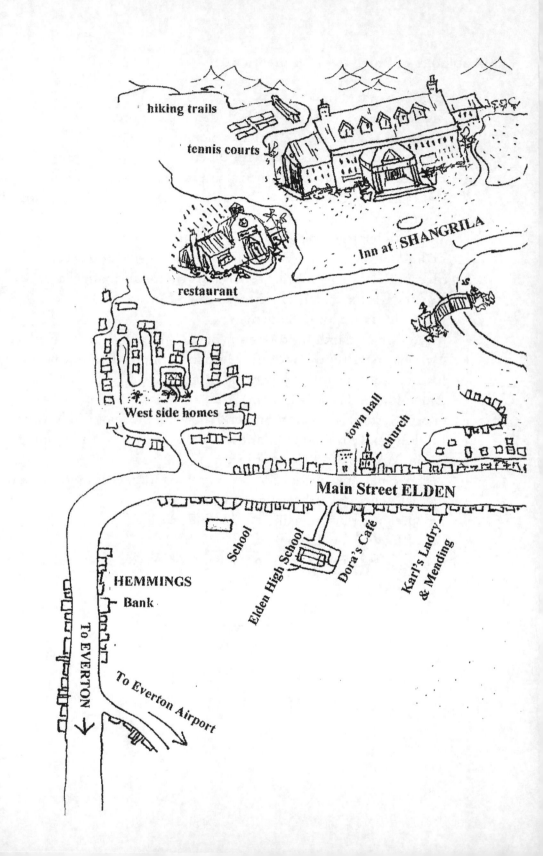

hiking trails

tennis courts

Inn at SHANGRILA

restaurant

West side homes

town hall

church

Main Street ELDEN

School

Elden High School

Dora's Café

Karl's Lndry & Mending

HEMMINGS

Bank

To EVERTON

To Everton Airport

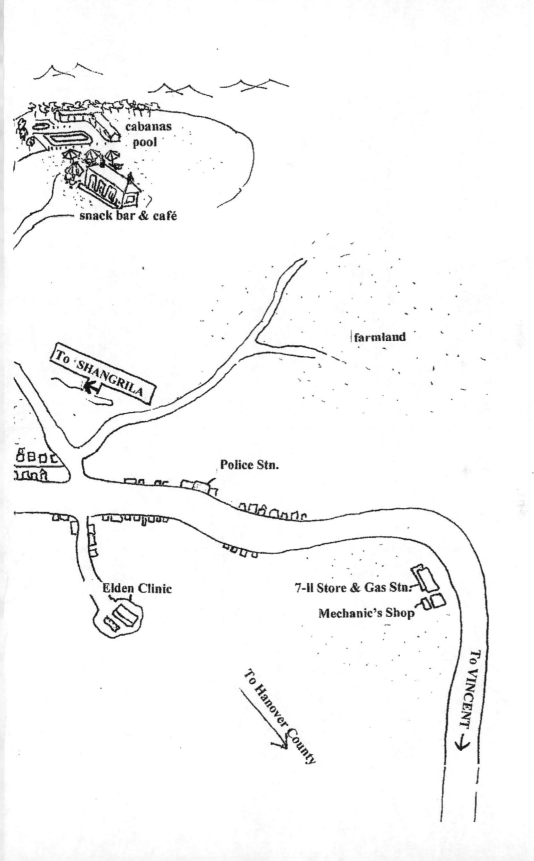

Chapter 1

It was not a pretty sight. Her lifeless body sprawled on the floor face down, with a scarf tightly wound and tied around her slender neck, upheaval in the small living room, all adequate and alarming evidence to tell the story of what had apparently gone wrong here. It was summer in Elden, early evening at dusk, windows open. Had anyone heard a scream? She had unmistakably been murdered and there appeared to have been a struggle. Her large shoulder bag lay unopened on the floor near the door, on top of a small string tied package, suggesting she had entered the apartment and dropped her things, not expecting an intruder.

The overturned table and two small chairs, framed photographs and table lamp lay broken in pieces on the floor near the window, clear evidence that once the door had been opened, she had been attacked, either by someone who had pushed in behind her, or was already in the room. There had been more than just a struggle although it did not appear to be a robbery. Boxes of clothing and an open suitcase which seemed to be serving as a drawer lay on the floor of the small bedroom. There was no furniture other than a single bed.

Jake, both the apartment manager and handyman, reported that he had discovered her body when he entered the apartment in the morning to install a smoke alarm as promised, and to leave a list of rules and information for the new tenant. He said he had knocked loudly for a few moments before entering, assuming the occupant was not there.

A muscular, dark haired man of about 40, Jake was the younger brother of the owner who had constructed the small two-unit apartment building three years earlier, replacing an older dilapidated house. He had been part of the construction crew, and was known and trusted by the other tenant in the adjacent apartment, a young woman who had been there just short of a year. When he saw the body face down on the floor just inside the door, he claimed to have hurriedly turned and run from the apartment, promptly calling the Police Department to report it.

The scene was next witnessed by Sgt. Mathew Reardon who had preceded Detective Kevin Branch across the threshold into the room. This was not the first case Matthew Reardon had been assigned to handle after having recently joined the Police Force in the county. It had not been long since he had graduated from the Police Academy at Victor, in Hanover County nearby. Prepared for experience in his newly acquired position as Sergeant, another murder case, especially involving this particular beautiful, young woman, was not what he had hoped for nor expected.

Sgt. Reardon and Detective Branch both stood motionless for a moment just inside the doorway surveying the details of the room, hesitant to begin the disagreeable job of examination, searching for fingerprints, evidence, and photographing the body before them. This was a small police station and these tasks, normally carried out by a team, were theirs alone to handle. It was also not the first time they had been called to work together. They now had a second homicide confronting them to deal with.

Chapter 2

It had been more than five years since Elena and her brother Frederik Vitki had returned to the small town of Elden where they had grown up, after learning their father had suddenly succumbed to an apparent heart attack and died. They were told that he had been out walking that afternoon, something he rarely did, which in itself had seemed odd to both of them.

He had been accompanied by his dog Cigar, who, whenever possible, was at his side. Why the dog had so curiously been named and where he had come from had never been explained as neither Frederik nor Elena had ever seen their father smoking a cigar. The dog, of uncertain ancestral origin and unknown background or age, may have been named by a former owner. In any case, Cigar had become an important companion to both of them during their years growing up in Elden in the way only a dog can be, although he was definitely their father's dog despite often being ignored by him, as he always ran loyally with a wagging tail to greet and acknowledge him as his master. He was, to Elena and Frederik, an affectionate little brown and white friend.

Their father had died on the street in front of the local Laundry & Mending Company and was buried in the local cemetery with no marker other than a small rough brown stone and a plastic crucifix that someone had thought to place beside it, unaware as to what, if any, religious conviction he may have had.

The burial had taken place within two days after his death before either of the two could manage to get there. There had been no mourners at the church cemetery, just the burial. The coroner had attributed his death simply to old age although some in Elden that had been aware of him and his penchant for drinking and staggering home from the local bars, had thought this diagnosis questionable. He had kept mostly to himself and was probably only about 65 as best as anyone knew. No birth certificate had been located nor required. Elden was for many in those days, just a small town on the way to someplace else. There were deaths from time to time but no murders that anyone knew of, or at least spoke about.

The news of her father's death reached Elena where she was working at a summer camp, generally acknowledged as being for disobedient teens. She had chosen to not check phone messages that day when all had gone hiking in the woods near the camp. When she finally returned and received the call, it was already too late in the day to find a replacement counselor, return to town and make arrangements to get to Elden, which she promptly did the following morning.

Her brother, Frederik had curiously offered no explanation as to why he had not responded in time to get there sooner which seemed strange, but she did not question him about it. He had received the call notifying him of his father's death, just as had Elena, from Karl Jenkins, who, since they had left town, had become the local Postmaster, proudly identifying himself by his new title when making the calls. He added that he had taken it upon himself to care for Cigar who had sat for three days in front of his business on the spot where their father had died. With a greying muzzle and limp, caused undoubtedly by arthritis in his hind legs, he had begun to show signs of old age years back and they were both surprised and pleased to learn that he was still alive.

Chapter 3

Karl Jenkins had run the local Laundry & Mending Company, so named by the former owner, after his own parents who had owned and operated it passed away, one soon after the other. He had always seemed strangely old when still a young man, as he had lost much of his hair prematurely, was nearly bald and wore rimless spectacles that may or may not have been prescribed specifically for him. Karl had completed high school with respectable grades and helped out part-time in the afternoons when school was over, expecting to eventually go away to college, but once he had begun to work full time after graduating, had never left town.

Over time, Karl had grown rather plump and often wore a pair of plaid slacks that appeared to have been inherited from someone along his family line who was substantially taller than he, as they were much too long for his short stature and bunched up in folds over his shoes. He wore various styles of colorful sweaters and a pair of brown and white saddle shoes that gave him the appearance of an ageing college student from times past. Consequently he fit well into the small rural community as yet another odd soul in the assortment of Elden inhabitants.

Karl's father, a slightly shorter version of Karl, had married his childhood sweetheart, both having grown up in town where it had been their dream to start the business they proudly operated on the main street of Elden. They had planted a sizeable vegetable garden behind their house just down the road although as they spent long days working at the laundry, their neighbor Vincent Delaney had often been seen watering and tending the garden while they were at work. It was assumed that he may have been paid something for this service, or more likely, benefited from some free laundry, dry cleaning and maybe even mending. No one had paid much attention nor particularly cared although the possibility of this arrangement had been duly noted. In any case, it did not appear that Vincent Delaney, along with many others in town, had much interest in his personal appearance or the status of his apparel and may not have felt that much laundering, dry cleaning or mending was particularly necessary or useful.

Some speculated that the garden should have been a job for Karl since he appeared not to have any outside activities, exercise, or interests to occupy him away from the job but they didn't contemplate the matter much beyond that. Cigar wound up following Vincent home one afternoon when he had stopped by to see Karl, and had remained with him which seemed satisfactory to both.

Chapter 4

The Dry Goods store which had once housed the small Post Office in a corner of the same building on Main Street had been closed and Karl Jenkins was awarded responsibility for conducting the local postal business which was then relocated to a small adjacent room and a corner of the countertop in his shop. Outgoing mail was picked up each afternoon more or less between 4:00 and 5:00 pm as well as in the two small neighboring communities, whenever the mail carrier arrived. The town was generally not first on the route.

The mail carrier, known only as Ted, drove a small grey indistinguishable car with a vinyl U.S. Postal Service sticker pasted crookedly on the passenger side door much too low to be easily read. He had clearly been entrusted with the responsibility of placing it on his car by someone at the regional postal authority and had obviously not measured nor planned where to place it once the adhesive backing was removed. No one had noticed nor been concerned about this discrepancy but simply recognized it as Ted's car when it appeared at the end of the day on one of the four weekdays that he came to collect and drop off the mail. Elden was a small town and the limited delivery and pick up arrangement was adequate if not excessive to everyone as there was rarely much outgoing mail to pick up or drop off. Ted nevertheless dutifully showed up more or less when expected and occasionally stopped to chat with Karl Jenkins or anyone else who might be around as well as on his days off when driving through town to Shangrila, the mountain resort where he worked part time.

Ted was not often seen out of his car other than his short stops at the newly appointed post office in the Laundry & Mending Company to pick up or deliver mail, although it had been noticed that he was unexpectedly tall and slender, and always appropriately attired as the local representative of the postal service, in that he wore a long sleeved grey shirt with an identifying postal logo on the right front pocket. He had become a regular in the comings and goings in Elden.

Things were what they were in town and had pretty much always stayed that way. No one had ever recalled a murder in Elden although noisy marital disputes were often overheard and thoroughly reviewed. Elena and Frederik's mother and father were often discussed in their deliberations, as neighbors did not fail to share evidence of any disorderly behavior.

It was not only Elena and Frederik who returned unexpectedly to Elden. Deciding to accept a job at the local Police Station in Elden after his graduation from the Police Academy, Mathew Reardon had also not expected to return, nor for there to be much challenge in his new position in town at the Police Dept., however, despite this, it was a new opportunity and a stopping off point for the time being. Their paths would cross again.

Chapter 5

The resort called Shangrila in the hills behind the town had been optimistically named by its owners who had come some years back to jointly open what began simply as a large, rustic, family-style restaurant. Eventually Shangrila began to draw business from the surrounding area once it was up and running, mostly for lack of anyplace else to go in the surrounding towns, and bit by bit was enlarged with the grounds and facilities significantly expanded and developed.

The Shangrila resort was high enough in the hills behind Elden to generally attract summer vacationers escaping the small and larger towns in the valley in search of the cooler temperature and the numerous activities and goings-on offered there. In addition, many of the townspeople found summer jobs at Shangrila once it had become established and expanded to include much more than the barn-like restaurant, which had been the initial undertaking. Eventually a smaller, less formal eating place was added, a small café-style restaurant and a snack bar by the pool and cabanas.

The two families that had joined in a partnership to purchase and begin the ambitious development of the thirty-two acre property had devoted their savings and energy to the venture. Once this undertaking had begun to be prosperous, expansion had begun, providing work for many in town as the property was cleared and more facilities added, until Shangrila was finally completed. It took no time before word spread and Elden benefited and grew, primarily due to the growing number of summer visitors passing through on the way to this newly discovered vacation getaway. Shangrila was becoming a desirable place to go in the entire region.

Initially there were jobs in the restaurant and once constructed and developed, in the sprawling inn, the café and snack bar, maintaining the large swimming pool, children's wading pool, tennis courts, landscaped grounds which included gardens and hiking paths, and overseeing the many other activities as well as adult and children's games. All told, this changed life in Elden considerably. Mathew Reardon had been one of many in town who had found part time work at Shangrila in a variety of capacities while he and his classmates were still in school.

Chapter 6

Ted, who for all anyone knew was unmarried, took delight in flirtations with the waitresses and girls he met at Shangrila on weekends when not delivering mail and where he worked longer days part time during the summer. He had, after watching her for some time, self-assuredly introduced himself one afternoon to an attractive blond named Sharon, having completed routine maintenance and cleaning of the swimming pool, his primary task there.

When not in his grey postal shirt, his attire familiar to most everyone in town, Ted appeared to be considerably more attractive, in fact, good looking in the shorts and blue Shangrila tee shirt he was required to wear as an identifiable uniform at work, which revealed his muscular physique and tanned body. His sandy colored hair, broad grin and friendly nature made him appealing to most who met him and he seemed a good fit for the job as well as being an eye-catching plus for the young girls who took note of him.

Chapter 7

Sharon Retton, who lived in town and had graduated from the local high school, had been hired to teach swimming and yoga to teenage girls that came for lessons after school and on weekends in addition to the inn's guests in a special program developed by the social director at Shangrila. This was her first job and she loved it. She had been hired ahead of four or five other girls who had applied for the position, having demonstrated both the personality and self-confidence they were looking for.

After swimming classes she often stayed on late into the afternoon to gossip, tease, and visit with the girls, helping some of them curl or braid their damp hair while others simply wrapped a towel around their head and sat to bask in the sun around the edge of the pool.

Ted enjoyed watching this giggling spectacle, and in particular seeing Sharon emerge from the pool in her light blue bikini, pulling off her bathing cap and seeing her blond hair fall to her shoulders. She too was lean, tanned and attractive and she knew it. He often made a point of being at the pool during her swimming lessons with the girls, either working or at least attempting to appear to be handling some phase of required maintenance.

Sharon was well aware of Ted's presence and obvious endorsement and felt comfortably safe with him watching her while surrounded as she was by the girls and others about. He had his work to do in any case and this was, after all, just a summer job for both of them. The flirtation had become rather mutually interesting and they began to anticipate the appearance of one another when classes took place or when Sharon would otherwise be at the pool on her own, a privilege granted by the Manager due to her position there.

Others who worked at Shangrila were also allowed to use the pool but only at specifically designated hours when it was unlikely there would be much opportunity and generally not a popular or desirable time for others to be there. As the schedule allowed for only those not currently on duty to use it during these hours, termed an "employee bonus" as the Manager liked to call it, this bonus went generally unused. This carte blanche freedom to use the pool whenever she so desired, caused Sharon to be largely unpopular among the other employees both for her often over-confident manner, and having been given the favored position that many others would have loved to have.

Chapter 8

Sgt. Mathew Reardon, with his dark hair and eyes, penetrating good looks and fit appearance after his physical training at the Police Academy and subsequent summer of relaxation, had been ready for something different which his new job provided, and he had been welcomed to the small Police Station a few miles down the road from the center of town where the small force had been inadequate due to the departure of one of the officers. There would then again be three to serve in the district.

Mathew was born at the local clinic in Elden, which also often served as a small local hospital, had grown up in town, graduated from high school and after working for several years on his father's farm, had moved away expecting it to be for good. He had proceeded to attend the Police Academy in Victor, across the border in Hanover County, south east of Elden, where he had recently graduated.

While there, just prior to completing his training, he had begun an intense affair with someone also from Elden which had ended abruptly and, after graduating, he purchased a late model, shiny black, pre-owned Mustang, wanting to get away and briefly explore beyond the borders of the county. He had needed and wanted a change. Returning to Elden had not been what he had initially expected to be doing. It had just happened that way.

During his last year of high school Mathew Reardon had occasionally been asked to assist the Physical Education instructor despite having no specific qualifications himself. However, as he had demonstrated his talents in outperforming others in sports, proven to be an exceedingly good athlete and team leader, and generally set a good example among his classmates, this role had become an important part of his school life. Having returned to Elden where his first employment opportunity had been to join the Police Department, he dropped by to visit his old friend, now the Baseball Coach, who enthusiastically urged him to return and assist with sports at Elden High School whenever time allowed.

This was an opportunity he readily accepted as it was appealing to be back at the school not only to supervise and engage in the sports activities he enjoyed, but also to reminisce about old times and appreciate, at least in some ways, being back at home. He welcomed the prospect, feeling it a pleasant diversion that would keep him busy at least for the time being. This would not be forever but at that time seemed to be a good decision.

Chapter 9

Rodney Kastor who hired Mathew was the regional Sheriff that also acted as the town Constable and had his office in the local Police Department. He was stout, red faced from years in the sun and had a girth not generally suitable for any kind of law enforcement work although his ready booming laugh and easy going manner was agreeable and he was well respected and relied upon to keep Elden safe. He had lived in town most of his life, loved to hunt and fish, undoubtedly much more than attending to the necessities of the safety of the community, and had at one time been manager of the restaurant at Shangrila. Nearly everyone in town had found their way there at some point in one capacity or another. Having known Mathew Reardon when he was younger and growing up in Elden, Rodney Kastor was glad to now have him on his staff at the Police Department. It was a good decision for both and one that would prove to be invaluable.

Chapter 10

Detective Kevin Branch who had come to work at the station only a year and a half earlier, enjoyed hunting as well, but mostly for thieves, shoplifters, pot and drug users, calling on noisy marital or barroom disputes, cornering peeping toms and in general making himself accessible to the surrounding communities for whatever disagreements or poor conduct might arise. He liked his position. Divorced and now free, he had found being tied down for too long to much of anything had not worked out well. For now, this was a good job for him and he did not need to feel pinned down due to his arrangement to cover the goings on in more than just one community.

Kevin was thirty-three, relaxed, self-assured and enjoyed meeting women although his looks could be considered ordinary. He was of average height and slight physique however he drew attention to himself by generally being smartly outfitted in a crisp, starched blue striped or yellow shirt and nicely creased slacks which he took regularly to the Laundry & Mending Company for dry cleaning and pressing. He often wore a bow tie and had a variety of what appeared to be expensive leather shoes, worn alternately in tan, brown or black to match the slacks chosen for that day. His hair was suspiciously nearly solid black, enhanced perhaps by some questionable coloring agent, and combed back into what could have been described as an out-of-date ducktail style.

This preoccupation with his looks and clothes as well as his fixation for women had been some of the chief reasons for Kevin's divorce and he was in no hurry to again complicate matters for himself but comfortable to wait and see whatever might develop that could be of interest.

Kevin appeared to keep pretty much to himself, disappeared for days at times and figured his cell phone was an adequate enough connection to whoever might need to reach him for the time being. He was nearly always available at any given time to respond to a call, possibly offering a new challenge or assignment, and as there were no requirements for either he or Mathew Reardon to report and remain all day at the small Police Station if otherwise engaged, felt relatively free to do as he pleased. This relaxed arrangement, enabled by new cell phones, suited him as well as Sheriff Kastor and Sgt. Reardon, and made it an appealing job, compared to one of more enforced attendance assumed undoubtedly to be necessary elsewhere. The informal set up at the Police Department also allowed Mathew Reardon the leisure time for the sports he had hoped for and he could often be found at the Elden High School enjoying being on the playing field with the students when not engaged in some form of police work or other diversion.

Chapter 11

A fourth at the small precinct was Henry Jordan who simply liked to hang around and be useful in the event he might be unexpectedly needed. Henry was thin with an angular face, long nose, slightly protruding ears, and greying sideburns that contrasted with his reddish-brown hair, all giving him the appearance of an ageing vaudeville entertainer. It was unknown how old he was to anyone other than possibly Sheriff Kastor, as everyone in town seemed to remember having seen Henry as far back as they could remember, always dressed in the same faded blue denim shirt and bib overalls with numerous pockets and various compartments in which he carried tools and whatever else he deemed important to carry about.

Like most of the men in town Henry could be called upon as a volunteer fireman although it was a rare occurrence when there was such a need. Having never created, pursued nor placed himself in front of any uncertain challenges, he had nevertheless found odd jobs as he had learned some carpentry, car maintenance and other indistinct repair work.

Henry usually looked as though he was in need of a good hot meal, and probably a bath, and was generally one of the first in line at the weekly church suppers where he may in fact have had his only nourishing meal that week. He lived by himself in two rooms behind the town's small hardware store, and walked just about everywhere as he had no car, catching a ride from time to time with the townspeople who stopped to give him a lift or with anyone who might be hiring him to do something.

Vague as Henry's place at the Sheriff's office might have been, it was acceptable to Sheriff Kastor who often sat with him in the small, simply furnished office to play cards and drink beer on a hot afternoon. He had, along with many others in town, made his way to Shangrila and at times managed to pick up some work there despite his lack of credentials or proof of experience, not to mention his unusual, untidy appearance. Once however, given a few small assignments by the manager who, not without some trepidation, had hired him, he proved to be not only able to do the job, but willing to take on work that had been unappealing to others and difficult to include in job descriptions. Henry was therefore kept on a temporary-employee call list and called on for jobs that he was likely to be able to handle. He found that being shown any form of appreciation for whatever he did was important and rewarding as having had few pats on the back in his lifetime, made him want to make every effort to please and do a good job. Working at Shangrila was a welcome opportunity to Henry who just got by. Despite his demeanor, no one had ever considered him dangerous or threatening in any way and he was, for the most part, unnoticed.

Chapter 12

Everyone in town watched their money, reluctant to entrust it to the Bank in Hemmings outside of town, or one of the two larger banks in Everton, which meant at least an hour's drive away. In addition, the fact that these were not local banks run by anyone that was known to the inhabitants of Elden, placed them under suspicion. Consequently it was thought by many that there may be hidden money or jewelry to be found on some of the properties in town although no one had ever been suspected or accused of trying to find it. Sheriff Kastor had not received any calls to report a theft, let alone a murder although there were many that had always kept a keen eye on who was out walking after dinner in the dark.

Neighbor watched neighbor in town and aside from the weekly church suppers on Sunday afternoons when most attended, offering a favorite homemade pie, dish or stew, heard the latest gossip and tasted one another's contributions, people kept pretty much to themselves. Some brought their home grown vegetables and wine to exchange on this occasion, generally leaving purchases at the stores to what were considered to be only necessary staples. This was how life was in the small town as well as in most other towns around, and no one seemed anxious to change things.

Chapter 13

The Town, having closed their small town-owned building that once served as both a small post office and dry-goods store, had leased the property to one of the oil companies. The Town Committee, as it was known, had agreed to the terms proposed and the oil company had promptly torn down the old building and erected a smaller one with wall space large enough to display automotive products, soft drink and snack machines, and had excavated and installed a gasoline pump out in front. This arrangement subsequently provided some much needed revenue to the town from the gasoline and oil sales, with a small percentage also from sales of related goods. It was an easy decision on the part of the Town Committee, as purchasing gas and oil had, until then, meant a sixteen mile drive down the road heading east away from Elden, to the Mechanics Repair Shop and adjacent gas station which also featured a fairly good sized 7-Eleven store.

Despite the addition of the new small gas station on Elden's main street, also known as Route 3, and the traffic it brought when nearby residents and others headed through town for the mountains and nearby Shangrila resort, the sixteen mile drive to the 7-Eleven store, despite the cost of gas, was often a popular destination for the town's younger generation as it also served to be what many considered a little get-away that could appear to be an innocent and acceptable outing, which, for the most part, it generally was.

Chapter 14

The 7-Eleven store was large enough to allow for a small bar at the side window where there were five or six stools available for anyone to stop, sit and sip a coke or beer and scratch off their lottery tickets while awaiting car repairs, or sometimes, for no reason at all. It was often the destination for first-time drivers, Mathew among them, who had practiced in their driveways and subsequently in the parking lot behind town hall, and eventually been allowed to drive to the 7-Eleven, generally with their fathers sitting anxiously in the back seat.

This was a much anticipated event for the town boys and Frederik had recalled his anguish at seeing those of his schoolmates relish their first opportunity to drive their father's cars on this much anticipated occasion. Elden held few opportunities for adventure or excitement.

Chapter 15

Growing up in town, Ellen and Frederik's family had no car, only their father's old dusty pickup truck loaded in the back with his farm implements and Frederik had hidden his depression and unhappiness with a quiet, solitary manner. This had enabled him to go unnoticed among the other boys at school who generally never failed to uncover, ferret out, and challenge any behavior they deemed suspicious or curiously interesting. This led to their many audiences in the principal's office for their actions, followed by a good deal of school window washing, repentant essay writing and janitorial duties as both punishment and reminder that bad behavior would not be tolerated. Smiling to himself, he had enjoyed seeing his classmates pay for their disagreeable performances, which he had hoped would be dealt with more severely, although he derived no gratification from any of it and in fact, by virtue of his own intent to separate from them, found himself to be at the same time, often isolated. He was thought by most to be a loner, had confirmed in his own mind that, in fact, he was, and had no desire to become anything else. His chief ambition was to escape from his unhappy, miserable home circumstances and leave town.

Elena, although a year older than Frederik, had assumed she was her brother's only ally when circumstances were rough at home although still young herself she could not fully understand his deepest feelings of resentment and longing to get away. This state of mind was something he had not completely defined within himself, and without the means to do anything about it, felt confined to a kind of holding cell, waiting to be released into what he assumed would be something better, but knew not what.

Chapter 16

The 7-Eleven store and gas station were run by Mr. & Mrs. Chandra and the adjacent Mechanics Repair Shop by their cousin, Mr. Sharma. They were referred to fondly by their customers as "the Charmers", most not knowing or ever inquiring as to their correct names although over the years the Chandras and Mr. Sharma had learned the names of most of their customers from the towns around and warmly greeted them by name. Mr. Chandra's wife had arrived from New Delhi, India to join him once the business had been established and they lived quietly and simply over the 7-Eleven in a small apartment, preparing a variety of sandwiches each day that could be microwaved on request and overseeing the sale of gas, soft drinks, beer, coffee, snacks, available notions and lottery tickets, which to many in and around Elden represented the equivalent of a stopover in Las Vegas. Coming to America and running their own business represented to them fulfillment of their own American Dream.

The Chandras were particularly always pleased to find willing and hopeful players to select from their unusually large assortment and mixture of lottery and scratch-off tickets, all prominently exhibited next to the cash register. They proudly displayed a card in the window announcing a $300.00 winner.

Chapter 17

Justin Haber's father Alden Haber had scratched off the ticket of one of the newest games and won $160.00. He had then promptly marched next door and enthusiastically arranged for the dent on the front bumper of his Toyota to be fixed, something he had begrudgingly not been willing to do since the accident. Mr. Sharma gave him an especially good price to repair it and Alden Haber, in appreciation, and still slightly overcome with his new windfall, bought a round of cold beer and sodas for everyone in the shop, including his son.

This unusual show of generosity appeared to be fundamentally out of character for Alden Haber, a big man in his late forties who towered over most others, was not particularly friendly, and rarely bothered to be polite. He, in fact, generally gave the impression of being in a perpetually bad mood and people stayed pretty much out of his way. He had married later in life and seen his only son Justin growing up to become, what for him, had so far been a disappointment rather than the son he had hoped to raise with enthusiasm and be proud of. He had not participated in nor made an effort to see many of Justin's school or sporting events, and had shown unjustifiable rage when grades were reported as merely passing. He had, in fact, expected a lot from his son and resented that he himself had so little influence over Justin's seemingly inadequate ability to set and achieve more meaningful goals. Consequently, there was little communication between them and Alden Haber felt no need to show him much, if any, affection.

Justin on the other hand had growing up concerns of his own which he had felt were his alone to deal with as his mother tended to entrust his discipline and welfare to his father, and there had been a steadily growing rift between them. He had recently been paroled by his father for a misdeed but reluctantly been given permission to drive occasionally to the 7-Eleven once he turned sixteen. Alden Haber who ordinarily paid for no extras, also had the car washed that day in the newly installed car wash which the Chandras had been paying on for more than a year. Alden and Justin then drove home. This had been an unusually positive day for both father and son.

Chapter 18

The Town Committee had finally decided to buy and install a proper mailbox in order to improve upon the informal pick up and drop off for mail at the Laundry. The mailbox had been placed prominently out near the curb in front of the building and Karl Jenkins was proud to oversee this installation although he had some concern that it might affect his ability to overhear and dispense gossip, as people no longer would be required to come in to drop off mail. As there was seldom much mail to be either dropped off or collected, this, to his dismay, nearly ended any postal traffic in and out of the shop.

The mailbox had no sooner been installed when Justin Haber had ploughed into it with his father's Toyota on the way to show off to Cecily Watson, a pretty blond that he had been admiring for some time. He was then not yet sixteen and Alden Haber was unaware that Justin knew how to drive, let alone taken his car out.

Unknown to his father, Justin had been secretly practicing on the road adjacent to their farm in the afternoons after school whenever the opportunity arose, in anticipation of making his driving debut in the presence of Cecily, whom he had prayed would be at home at the time to witness this significant event. It was a Saturday afternoon when he knew both his parents and hers should still be at work as mostly everyone in town that could worked on Saturdays in an effort to make ends meet.

Alden Haber who had plumbing and electrical repair training and experience was on call at Shangrila that day and had caught a ride as he often did with anyone in town who had a regular job there. This saved money on gas although it was thought unlikely, unless asked, he would either volunteer to drive or offer to pay for anyone else's gas. He kept to himself and those who knew of his temper, how unforgiving and demanding he was with his son, stayed away from him whenever possible.

Fortunately it was only the mailbox at the edge of the sidewalk that was demolished and not the Laundry window, by then officially the Post Office a few feet beyond, that would have been damaged as well.

Justin had been aptly punished at home and put on probation, with the keys to the car from then on placed in what seemed an unlikely to be discovered hiding place; the teapot on the kitchen window sill. No one had ever used it for tea as it had been handed down and therefore considered an antique not to be used. This new repository replaced the hook on the back door for the key, as Justin had clearly found the key, when plainly in sight, much too overwhelming a temptation and opportunity to overlook. When obtaining the key thereafter from the teapot, it was made certain by Alden Haber that Justin was not within eyesight and out of the kitchen until such a time as he would be given proper permission to drive.

Chapter 19

Sunday was a day off in Elden for those who chose to go either to church followed by the potluck supper, get drunk or visit nearby relatives. Everyone in town seemed to know everyone else or at least who they were and their business, so going to visit relatives was an opportunity to spread gossip beyond the limits of the town and generally enjoy a good Sunday meal at other's expense while doing so.

Farm land was readily available in the region as the sons and daughters that had grown up in Elden, such as Mathew Reardon, had been expected to carry on with farming and planting as had their parents and grandparents, but were only too anxious, as Elena, Frederik and others had been, to get away.

Mathew Reardon being one of the older town boys who had not felt he wanted to remain in Elden to carry on with his family farm, was often seen driving out of town, and on some occasions, with Sharon Retton. This had been noted by many and particularly by Elena.

Chapter 20

On the occasion of Elena's return to Elden after her father's death, there had been little change since she and Frederik had left and they were faced upon arrival in town with what they knew lay ahead. They both swiftly moved to take care of what needed to be done which primarily involved cleaning and clearing out the small two bedroom house where they had grown up. The opportunity to learn more about Frederik's life since they had both left, along with news of Mathew Reardon was soon to come.

Most of the few friends they had known in childhood were assumed to have long since left town, and they made no effort to find or see them while there, as there was work to do, although Elena had secretly imagined running into Mathew Reardon and hoped it would happen. She had not stopped thinking about him since leaving Elden four years earlier and fantasized they would somehow meet again and be together some day. In any case, their reception in town had not been noticeably warm nor welcoming, with few friendly or caring faces to greet them. It seemed to both Elena and Frederik that they had been gone long enough to have become uninteresting, if remembered at all, and especially with their father now gone. This last visit to Elden represented presumed closure at the time to both of them.

While working to clear out the house and reliving some moments of nostalgia recalling the frustrations of growing up, they found photographs of some of their schoolmates now in dusty boxes in the attic. In looking through them, both admitted to having had crushes on a few. Elena confessed to Frederik that when younger, she had once met Billy Ellison behind the tool shed and received her first kiss. Billy had, as she recalled, been very intent on pointing out their physical differences, information which he had obtained largely by peeking through the bedroom window after dark at the Folsons who lived next door to his family, and had, thereafter, continued to seek out any and all other similar, obtainable opportunities, committed to increasing this stimulating evidence.

When older, Elena's biggest infatuation had been for Mathew Reardon, which she had soon realized, added her to the list of a large number of girls who were also attracted to him and he made no effort to hide it. She had kept this to herself, her own secret fixation and Mathew had definitely not faded from her memory or her thoughts.

Frederik was rather quiet and somewhat reluctant to talk about some of the girls that he had known and liked that had not always responded to him as he might have hoped during his unhappy growing up years as an Elden teenager. He had assumed at times, that they perceived him to have been the son of the town drunkard. For this reason, he allowed himself to find odd justification for their lack of interest or negative reaction to him, although Frederik was, in fact, in Elena's opinion, nice looking and, being quiet, could seem at times aloofly mysterious. This together with his indiscernible manner had ironically attracted a few girls whom she suspected he may have been taking full advantage of at the time.

He had only once shared his innermost feelings with his sister regarding his crush on the pretty, blond, Sharon Retton, who was lively, popular, and a year older than he. He had been smitten by her looks and outgoing carefree personality and Elena supposed he secretly may have imagined himself to be her boyfriend. She also assumed that Sharon was probably unaware of his presumably masked interest, or even particularly aware of him, although their neighbor, Mrs. Hancock, one of the few people that showed any kindness towards them, had once revealed that she had observed Sharon walking down the road past the house on more than one occasion. This had seemed odd to Elena in that Sharon lived at the other end of town.

Elena who was not particularly good looking as was Sharon or for that matter her brother Frederik, had nevertheless, a sense of purpose, stood up straight and kept her pretty, long brown hair tidily styled and pinned up, all of which combined to give her an orderly, assured, neat and confident appearance. She had herself in fact, on more than one occasion, purposefully walked home from school or work at the Clinic detouring off the main road in order to pass Mathew Reardon's house. As it was set somewhat back from the road on the large farm his family owned, it had seemed unlikely that he would spot her from a window.

Chapter 21

Once having gone through the process of cleaning out the house and doing all they could do, Elena and Frederik posted a For Sale sign in front of the house which was close to the main road, the one acre lot being mostly in the rear. The weeds had taken over the small vegetable garden which, as children, they had once taken pride in planting and tending, with the rest of the land behind the shed by now uncared for and dry as it had been for so long. At one time there had been corn planted in the field behind the house which Frederik and Elena sold during the summer from a small table they set up by the road in front of the house.

Most of their father's tools, once necessary for his work on the nearby farms, were now rusted or broken, and they found little in the house worth salvaging. The furniture, mostly second hand, was left for whoever would next own the property to either discard or use as they pleased. They were glad to be outside in the fresh air again once the job was completed. Both felt there had been little of sentimental value worth keeping.

They made their way to the town garage designated as a donation drop-off depot for no-longer-needed-belongings and left whatever might still be useful for someone to find. The few other possessions of any value, most having belonged to their mother, were left at the church in the drop box set up for this purpose in the vestibule. Goods collected were meted out to those in need by the eighty-six year old town elder entrusted with the position, which appeared to be his most significant responsibility. He seemed to have little use for much of anything other than chewing tobacco and whatever whiskey he was offered and there was scant likelihood he would be tempted to take for himself anything donated. They had, sadly, few mementos to take away with them.

Finally they placed an ad in the two daily papers, offices which were in the town hall buildings in Hemmings and Everton, the two largest towns nearby, the 7-Eleven, and gas station, plus the town hall in Elden. The keys were left with Karl Jenkins at the Laundry and he agreed to bring any and all prospects to open and show the house and property in an effort to sell it. He was also promised a generous commission provided he successfully found a buyer, made all the necessary arrangements for passing of title and deed with the town clerk, and would see to all details which they had not wanted to return to handle. They finally made time to sit together and catch up after so many years before leaving again, as at that point in time, neither had any desire to be returning to Elden. This was not to be so.

Chapter 22

Sharon Retton had been a cheerleader at the local high school and seemed to have a sense of purpose and sureness beyond other girls her age and in her classes which was obvious to everyone who knew her, including her teachers.

During the summer Sharon generally had managed to name the jobs of her choice at Shangrila where most of the other girls who applied often found themselves behind the scenes washing dishes, cleaning or making beds. Finally securing the coveted position of teaching swimming to teens, it had allowed her the opportunity to be seen often which appealed to her personal requirements. She was popular with boys in school and with some of the older boys she encountered in town that she often found to be considerably more fascinating, one of whom was Mathew Reardon. Sharon had been seen often in town by many who noted that she appeared to have little apparent supervision. Not much passed the eyes and ears in the town unnoticed.

Her Mother, Gloria Retton, also a strikingly attractive woman who caught the eye of most men she passed, was believed to have a job in the next county as she left in her silver-blue Ford convertible early most mornings and returned, as far as anyone could see, during the evening hours just before or shortly after her husband, Bill Retton returned from the bank in Hemmings, five miles down the road southwest of Elden. She had been noticeably observed, as had her daughter Sharon, by most of the inhabitants of Elden.

The Rettons lived in one of the largest houses at the West end of town, thought to be the "rich" side, with a meticulously groomed lawn and long driveway, embraced at the entrance by two tall narrow stone pillars with large and rather dramatic torch lights atop each. The house, which had caused quite a stir while under construction, had the full attention of everyone in Elden. Some of the town boys had been able to find work under the supervision of the construction manager, a splendid chance for them to learn a range of jobs while also catching an occasional glimpse of Sharon and her mother. There hadn't been many opportunities before the construction of Shangrila for the boys in town to find work and on-the-job training and this was a welcome break for them.

Once completed, the Retton's house was, without question, an impressive, although rather inappropriate, addition to the small town, and fascinated all who purposefully passed by to see it. The house which had been designed by a newly licensed, and therefore inexperienced, young architect in Hemmings, appeared to have been initially conceived as an elegant farmhouse, but in its many stages of redesign and construction had, one at a time, acquired innumerable additional decorative motifs at the whim of the young designer, so that, upon completion, it appeared to be an attempt at recreating a smaller rural version of a southern mansion while straining to retain an innovative, but impressive, badge of simplicity. Mr. Retton was not pleased with the ostentation that had ensued since his approval of the original design, but said nothing as his wife Gloria was overjoyed with the dramatic outcome.

Soon other homes, although less pretentious and smaller but equally ambitious, began to spring up in the same neighborhood, which eventually grew to become known as the prosperous section of Elden. Many abandoned houses and old, unused storefronts in the area were torn down and vacant land developed, as those seeking less expensive land to build upon had discovered these opportunities in quiet Elden.

With her parents both away during the day and often well into the evening, Sharon Retton had limited supervision and was seen out often at different times of the late afternoon and evenings with most of the boys in town who were currently popular. Her many admirers were generally more than willing to meet her if only to be seen briefly with her whenever the opportunity arose, despite knowing they were not necessarily her first choice.

Given all the attention she received, it was instinctively more fascinating for Sharon to tease anyone whom she felt may not have admired or worse yet not noticed her. One of many who had seemed to fall into this category had been a nice looking but seemingly awkward young man in the class a year behind her in school named Frederik, who had at one time caught her eye.

It had seemed, disappointingly to Sharon, that he was unaware and even disinterested in her, although she could not be certain, and pretended to ignore him when passing, fully confident that he would eventually follow with the same performance of her other admirers who attempted in some way to make themselves known to her, hoping for at least recognition. When this had not readily happened, she made a point of learning where he lived and curious about him, had once or twice walked along the street passing his small, modest house while intentionally appearing to disregard it, looking the other way. His apparent disinterest was, she recognized, a new experience for her and one that intrigued her as she considered this diffidence toward her to be oddly appealing.

Chapter 23

Like many others in town, including his Father Alden who was employed at Shangrila, Justin Haber had also begun to work there part time during his last year in high school with the agreement that he would do what was needed whenever he arrived to report for duty. This was more than a satisfactory arrangement for him as it was an opportunity to work in different positions without being isolated in any particular routine job that he may not have found to his liking.

He had found that in addition to his comparable freedom in not being required to be in one place at all times, he was able to sneak Cecily Watson into the pool area from time to time to enjoy a swim. Having entertained her on more than one occasion in the back seat of his father's car in addition to their frequent rendezvous elsewhere whenever possible, this had resulted in a strikingly more positive relationship between them and she came for a swim often during the hot summer, quietly slipping into the water and then tanning herself by the poolside with a book, headphones and a soft drink beside her.

With a towel wrapped around her head after emerging from the pool and within the same age group as most of the girls there taking lessons, she had felt she could go largely unnoticed and had reported this to Justin who was relieved to hear it. Having taken this liberty, it appeared that she had not been observed, in which case he could lose his job. He had however urged her to go whenever possible at times when there were fewer girls at the pool as she would be less likely to be questioned. Cecily, grateful for the opportunity, agreed this made sense.

Justin had become as passionately obsessed with Cecily as he had with saving his earnings to put towards one day buying his own car, and requested additional hours whenever available to work during the summer months, always the busiest time of year at Shangrila. His car would be bigger and nicer than his father's Toyota.

Chapter 24

Years ago when they had first arrived in Elden, Frederik and Elena had rapidly begun to feel their family was looked down upon and not welcome. Their dad's father who spoke only broken English arrived with them, having nowhere else to go, and slept in the large shed out back which had been carefully cleaned out by their mother and made into a just barely adequate, but tolerable, sleeping room with a curtain at the window and a small heater for cold nights. He worked alongside their father and drank nightly alongside him as well at one of the two local taverns, verbally abusing just about anyone within earshot for what most folks in town felt was for no good reason. While growing up, their father's angry and loud behavior to all was observed by neighbors and others in town and caused both of them to have more a sense of shame than embarrassment. They kept largely to themselves, dreaming and imagining that they would someday run away.

Their mother had failed to remember where she lived one day when walking home from wherever she had wandered off to and wound up in a neighbor's cow shed a few doors away where she remained, quietly undiscovered, until she succumbed to pneumonia and died a few days later. Their father had simply buried her next to his cherished sunflowers in the back yard before telling anyone, and was drunk by the time the ladies who diligently attended the local church, and thought highly of themselves for having done so, obligingly appeared, having learned what had happened. They arrived bearing a few hastily prepared home-made dishes, and what they undertook to be the appearance of appropriate sympathy. The ladies soon left hurriedly, anxious to deliberate on the condition of the inside of the house which no one had ever seen, and to discuss the situation in detail.

While their anguished childhood, their father's alcoholism and mean temper plus their mother's inability to cope with either him or the responsibility of raising the two children had been evidenced by nearly everyone in town at some point, despite having kept their distance for years, the ladies who had arrived agreed unanimously that at that point, it was closure to it all.

Chapter 25

Justin Haber had not seen Cecily Watson for several weeks and called her suggesting they drive over to the 7-Eleven to say hello to the "Charmers", grab a lottery ticket and have a beer.

Justin picked Cecily up just after lunch, in time to go and return before the afternoon traffic swelled, and as she got into the car which Justin now had permission to drive when his Father was either not working or had grabbed a ride to Shangrila, she asked him to pull over once on the road out of town. It was there that Cecily announced abruptly that she was certain she was pregnant and promptly burst into tears while Justin simultaneously absorbed the enormity of what she was telling him and also burst into tears, having no other immediate release. They both sat in silence for some moments by the side of the road, certain that drivers passing them in their cars must be staring at them through the window knowing precisely what conversation had just transpired. Justin put his arm around Cecily in a tentative, hesitant manner, not knowing what he could say, turned the car around and began to drive slowly back to Elden in silence, both of them feeling their worlds had just collapsed.

Chapter 26

Elena had left home at 17, almost a year after Frederik had left, having graduated from high school and taken with her savings from working at the Elden Clinic, Shangrila in Summer, and Dora's Café & Coffee Shop. There she had worked at various jobs, assisting the cook whenever Dora's helper hadn't shown up, and whenever asked to come and lend a hand.

Dora was a sweet, buxom, rosy-cheeked woman in her late 50's who had never married and had learned to cook from her ageing parents when they ran the small café, and had continued on when they were no longer able to do so. She had more than just a few cats at home which regularly left random quantities of fur in different shades on Dora's clothing that required brushing off each morning upon her arrival at work.

This activity was seldom ever completed before the hustle and bustle of running the café took precedence. The early morning customers seemed unconcerned about the bits of fur drifting off Dora's apron as she rushed about the coffee shop seeing to her customers, serving coffee, while shouting orders across the small café to the cook, whose small galley kitchen space was barely concealed behind a bank of shelves where dishes and glassware were stacked.

Many of the young people in Elden, not anxious to return home immediately after school, stopped by at Dora's small soda fountain counter and found her always ready to listen to their problems, provide advice along with freshly squeezed lemonade in summer or, in cold weather, hot cocoa and a chocolate chip cookie for fifty cents. She was an important personality with soul to many in town which some recognized then and many more so later.

Mathew Reardon had, at one time, helped out in the kitchen, and the turnout of girls after school, his obvious admirers, had swelled noticeably. Elena had been one of those girls, and had then quietly and successfully managed to be hired by Dora after school, hoping for the opportunity to work alongside Mathew in whatever capacity might become available. This placed her in a position she felt was superior to the "counter girls" who would sit sipping a soda often for an hour or more, although due to the pressures of producing the customer's orders in the limited space, it had disappointingly neither resulted in her finding much opportunity to get to know Mathew better nor for him to recognize or distinguish her from the others as she would have liked.

Chapter 27

Mr. & Mrs. Chandra has been looking forward to a weekend at Shangrila which had been planned for some time once they knew their niece Nelam would be coming from India for a school vacation. As there was little else to do nearby and they wanted to avoid the daily driving time to the next County of Hanover despite that there was a museum, theatre and restaurants plus a miniature golf course among other things to do, they had decided to splurge on a visit to Shangrila.

Nelam Chandra had been thrilled when she learned of the opportunity to visit her Aunt and Uncle in America and once the suggestion had been made to her family in New Delhi by the Chandras, the entire family had set about to make it happen. Having already saved a substantial amount of money for Nelam's college tuition, it had been decided by the family that this trip to America could be justified and considered a part of her learning experience as well as an additional somewhat related form of education, and it was all they could talk about despite the disappointment of learning it would not be near New York or Hollywood given the distances in America. Instead, this was a small, rural community, pretty much in the middle of nowhere although it was more than fine for Nelam who would have the chance to spend time with her favorite Aunt and Uncle as well as her first trip away from her family for a much longed-for visit to America before starting college.

Chapter 28

Eighteen years earlier, Gloria, Sharon's mother, had just turned seventeen when she was married in Hemmings, less than a year after her high school graduation. She had grown up there and met Bill Retton when she had taken her savings and gone to the local bank to eagerly apply for her very first account. Bill was, at that time, a promising, young, newly appointed, Assistant Bank Manager and had been filling in that day at the front desk as he often enjoyed doing when the New Accounts Manager, whose desk faced the front door, was away. When Gloria walked purposefully in at ten o'clock that morning, wearing a new pair of high heels and a soft peach colored cotton dress that revealed her shapely figure, Bill Retton was smitten. Although he had noticed her in town on various occasions, he had been habitually focused on his studies and career, until that morning.

He began to call on Gloria persistently, showering her with gifts, taking her to any and all of the most expensive restaurants around and proposed to her within a few months, having obtained her father's willing and enthusiastic approval. Bill Retton was thought to be a good catch despite being seven years older than Gloria, and neither she nor her father saw any disadvantage whatsoever to this age difference.

Once married, they lived in town in the small house owned by his parents only a few miles from their own until she became pregnant with Sharon. A sprawling two acre property on the western side of Elden, five miles away, had become available and it was decided that with some help from his parents, together with a mortgage loan at a preferred rate from the bank, it would be a good investment for them, a new place to build their first home and raise children, as well as an opportunity to separate themselves somewhat from the family and a life that was, in fact, becoming too routine and too confining for Gloria. This was arranged and a young talented architect hired to draw up plans for what they both eagerly anticipated would be something unique in a custom designed new home for themselves. This had been years ago. A lot had happened since then.

Chapter 29

Once the new mailbox in front of the Laundry & Mending Company had been ordered and installed and the old one taken to the town depot for probable salvage, the parking space in front was once again kept clear for Ted to park while collecting and dropping off mail. Karl Jenkins had noted to someone at that time that he hadn't seen Ted for a while although he generally either stopped briefly to chat or at least honk or wave when making his mail rounds. He was working longer hours by then at Shangrila although had managed to complete his scheduled postal rounds. Not much thought was given to it as with the limited amount of mail that generally passed through the town, days could in fact go by with no notice of any reduction, lack or excess in its volume.

Chapter 30

Arriving in Everton's small airport, Nelam's Uncle, Ranjit Chandra, was there to meet her and they drove back the sixty plus miles through Hemmings to Elden where they stopped at Dora's Café for a lemonade, before heading east, the last sixteen miles, arriving at the 7-Eleven just after dark. It was that same evening after dinner, once they had settled down to catch up, that the Chandras, no longer able to postpone their news, revealed their big surprise which was to spend a week together at the nearby resort called Shangrila where Nelam would have a chance to swim, meet other girls, join in hiking and other activities and have a special vacation experience while in their care. The Chandras were enthusiastically looking forward to their stay there as well, as it meant a much needed vacation for them. All the arrangements had been made and paid for in advance. This was to be a wonderful reunion and adventure for all three of them.

The next day, as Nelam recovered from her long trip from India, she unrolled the colorful Punjabi outfits she'd chosen to bring and presented gifts of sandalwood incense and handmade jeweled pillow cases to the Chandras. They then packed their suitcases into the car, gave instructions to Mr. Sharma regarding the details and particulars of running the 7-Eleven store, explaining the vast display of lottery tickets available, and drove to Shangrila where they checked in. Nelam was thrilled with the surprise and they all settled in and began to bask in the luxury of being served all their meals, a hearty buffet breakfast each morning with a variety of juices, fruits, hot and cold cereals, eggs in any style, bacon and sausages, choice of pancakes or waffles, sweet rolls, jams and jellies, all followed later, whenever they chose to enjoy it, a light lunch with selections from a large salad bar, sandwiches, hamburgers, hot and cold drinks, luscious desserts made at the inn, and more. They could decide to eat at the inn's more formal restaurant or at the café and snack bar by the pool where midday teas, coffees and cookies were available and tempting along with a variety of sandwiches and cold drinks. There was swimming as well as tennis which both Nelam and her uncle had grown up playing in New Delhi, and the opportunity to sign up to play with other guests in doubles or on their own. Each evening after a day of activity and an occasional nap, they looked forward to the appetizing, varied and delicious dinners offered at the inn, which they enjoyed despite the lack of curry seasonings they generally considered essential to most meals. Trying out different dishes from the large, varied menu was a luxury they relished.

In addition to the planned activities, they took pleasure in taking strolls around the garden paths that had been beautifully landscaped with flowering trees and a large variety of plants including seasonal colorful begonias, snapdragons, day lilies, verbena, hibiscus, and an abundance of bright yellow roses which surrounded the buildings as well. During the evening in the large activities room at the inn, bingo, bridge and other games were available. There was also a feature film shown nightly after dinner, especially popular with those who may not have shown interest in playing games. It was turning out to be a wonderful vacation for the Chandras and for their niece Nelam.

Chapter 31

Dr. Gregory had run the Elden Clinic in Elden for many years, which served as hospital, out-patient clinic, veterinary hospital and more. He had recognized Elena's attention, curiosity and eagerness to learn some basic skills when she was fourteen and there for a few days with measles. Her interest had been prompted not only from wanting to learn how to do something, but to be away from home as much as possible, and she was never certain if Dr. Gregory had guessed this and possibly heard rumors about her unhappy home life. Whether this was the case or not, he encouraged her to come often once she had recovered, and had taken time to see that she had chores on the days when she often showed up after school. The experience and knowledge gained at the Clinic were also a wonderful escape which Elena found later to be invaluable.

Mathew Reardon had also found part time work at the clinic after school on many occasions and Elena found herself watching for him at every opportunity. Those days had been happy ones for her although she was not unaware that her interest and crush on Mathew had seemingly gone unnoticed by him.

Later, after leaving Elden, Elena found an opportunity to work in a small clinic similar to where she had first received her informal training with Dr. Gregory at the Elden Clinic. Like Mathew Reardon who also dreamed of leaving Elden to pursue his own dream and enroll at the Police Academy, her hope had been to go to college, and she set out to make it happen, working at whatever part time jobs she found available in addition to her work at the clinic, attending classes at night, and studying with little time or money for much else. She had not stopped thinking about Mathew and felt somehow their paths would meet again. Aware that he had been seeing Sharon Retton, Elena's determination to succeed took precedence at that point in her life although Mathew Reardon continued to be her fantasy on hold.

Dr. Gregory had written a letter of recommendation which had been her most precious possession, and which proved to be more than helpful in finding work. With his letter in hand plus hard work, she had known she would continue and succeed in reaching her goal. Elena and Mathew were alike in many ways, both coming from the small, confining town of Elden with its seemingly limited future, and driven by the same determination to get away and accomplish something for themselves.

When Elena finally completed what she had set out to achieve, nearly five years had seemingly passed quickly while she had worked, studied and obtained a degree in Social Services. Her hope was to continue to work with youngsters who had probably experienced the same or similar unhappy home life that she and Frederik had. They had both gone their separate ways after leaving home, had not been in touch and now, both back in Elden, were glad for the opportunity to catch up with each other.

Frederik unfortunately had no such mentor during those early years, but had changed dramatically from the thin, quiet boy he had been at sixteen, to a self-possessed and seemingly confident young man. At first, he seemed reluctant to try to explain his years away, although it was clear that he was ready to now open up and share his experiences with his sister. They had both escaped from what had been an unhappy childhood and had only each other to turn to. Much was yet to come.

Chapter 32

There had been a "bit of trouble" at Shangrila as it was briefly noted by the local paper and until it could be determined just what had in fact happened and then reported in full sensational detail, no one seemed to know what had taken place and could only speculate on the matter as it was being kept quiet by the Manager and those employees loyal or smart enough to not speak about it and possibly lose their jobs.

Sgt. Reardon and Detective Branch had been seen driving hurriedly through town early in the evening the day of the incident and while many watched for their return and some news of why they had been summoned, they had not been seen again that day. Curiosity grew and as it appeared to be the first incident of any kind to draw suspicion or interest in the goings on at Shangrila, incited neighbors to communicate with one another more than usual, all hoping to be the first to hear of any news or gossip they could report.

Chapter 33

It had happened quietly at the end of the afternoon when everyone had, one by one, left the pool and gone in to change for dinner and the evening's entertainments. Reluctant to move away from the paradise of her spot at the poolside where she had spent most of the afternoon swimming, reading and just daydreaming, she had not noticed that she was suddenly alone nor had she seen her attacker approaching as she had bent to put her book and sunglasses in the small drawstring bag she had brought with her. Feeling the first chill of the approaching evening, she had wrapped her towel around her small frame and tucked it in at the waist leaving the turban towel on her head, while looking forward to a hot shower and drying her hair back in the comfort of her divine room. She'd had a wonderful three days at Shangrila. They were Nelam's last.

Chapter 34

Gloria Retton had desired the silver-blue Ford convertible with cream color leather seats from the minute she had laid eyes on it in the Ford showroom in Everton. While Bill Retton, who, by nature, was somewhat conservative and, in fact, drove an older Chevrolet himself lest he be thought to be prospering from his role as Bank Manager, proclaimed his reluctance to buy it for her, but had nevertheless gone with her to purchase it and select the extras, including additional speakers and a separate hard top to use in Winter. This was a happy moment for Gloria Renton who had already envisioned herself sailing down the road in this lovely blue dream of an automobile. The white two-door car she had been driving since shortly after she and Bill were married, Bill's first gift to her, was then traded in. She had never complained but had secretly disliked driving what had seemed to her to be a utilitarian and unstylish car. This was now more Gloria Retton's style.

Bill had already recently succumbed to his daughter Sharon's beseeching requests for her first car which after much debate had evolved from being something to just-get-around-in to a slightly used, but therefore upgraded, model. The purchase of these cars for both mother and daughter represented, for him, the ever-increasing lack of control he had over either one of them, in addition to not knowing their whereabouts a good deal of the time.

Returning from the bank late each evening, he was pleased to be back in the comfort of his home, although neither Sharon nor Gloria were generally there to greet him. Putting his feet up, fixing himself a scotch, and dozing off with the evening paper was for the time being all that he required. This was not always however his only scotch. Bill Retton had begun to not look well for some time.

Chapter 35

It was nearly five o'clock that afternoon when the Chandras were just concluding a nap in their room when the Manager together with Sgt. Mathew Reardon had knocked on their door with the visit they had both dreaded making. Sgt. Reardon was the first to speak, telling them that their niece, who had apparently stayed on alone and unnoticed after her swimming lesson when the other girls staying at the inn had gone in to shower and change for supper, had been found strangled in front of the changing rooms, next to the pool.

After a long, heartbreaking and painful conversation with the Manager and Sgt. Reardon, who, on behalf of the other officers, had been designated to tell them what had taken place, the Chandras agreed to speak to no one about it until they had again been contacted by Sgt. Reardon, who promised to make a full investigation and find the answers they so desperately needed as soon as possible.

The Chandras, overcome with grief, learning their niece had been slain, remained inside their room that evening and again all the following day, unable to face anyone, and desperate to understand how and why this shocking and dreadful thing could have taken place. Finding the killer seemed to Sgt. Mathew Reardon to be more easily promised than might be accomplished, although he assured them that everything possible would be done to find who had murdered their niece and why it had happened. The Chandras could only wait to learn what they, in fact, were anything but anxious to hear.

Sgt. Reardon urged the Manager and Assistant Manager to keep the shocking matter quiet until it could be thoroughly investigated, as nothing like this had ever happened at Shangrila and they were all well aware that its reputation could be ruined beyond repair if this became known in town and to the press.

The majority of employees working that day were in fact unaware of what had happened and only a few who knew, as well as the Chandras, were instructed to say nothing until it could be determined just what had happened and who was responsible. Sgt. Reardon and Detective Branch had their work to do. This murder they had been called on to investigate needed to be solved in as short a time as possible. It was the most dreadful day ever for the Chandras and for Shangrila and not a good day for Mathew Reardon or Kevin Branch.

Chapter 36

Elena and Frederik, having been out of touch during the five years since both had left Elden, had a lot to learn about each other, and Frederik was clearly anxious to share his experiences with his sister.

He commenced in telling her about the day five years ago when he left Elden, and had thumbed a ride to the 7-Eleven, and there met a van driver who was in the process of delivering furniture to an address in Victor, a town across the border in the next county, a little over a two hour trip. Glad for some company and feeling some empathy for the troubled young man he had just met, the driver Bob had asked no questions and invited Frederik to hop in and join him for the ride. This was to be the beginning of more than just a short trip but a journey that Frederik was sorely in need of.

They finally arrived in Victor, after stopping briefly along the way for hot dogs and coffee. Bob had begun to recognize Frederik's obvious predicament after conversing with him during their ride together, and that he was in serious trouble. While he did not push him for details, he could see that he was beginning to feel some responsibility towards his young, anxious companion and Frederik, sensitive, unsure of himself, and aware of his uncertain dilemma, appreciated the attention and concern.

Bob effortlessly located the address where they were to deliver the furniture and pulled up at precisely the time expected in front of a handsome Colonial house in Vincent with a well-manicured lawn, prominent, colorful flower beds on either side of the front door and handsome stone fencing bordering the property. There were towering lamps along the street in what was clearly a well maintained and pristine neighborhood. Frederik felt glad to have been able to remain with Bob in the van.

As they arrived, an attractive middle aged couple stepped outside the house to greet them, inviting them, as they alighted from the front cab of the van, to have a cold drink before unloading. They were warm and friendly and seemingly unhurried as they proceeded to bring out a tray bearing cold iced tea in tall glasses and a plate of home-made cookies, offering that they had relocated to their new home only six months earlier. Now, comfortable in their new community, with Frank Grayson firmly established in his new position in town, they had decided to remove the last of their household possessions from storage and had sent for them.

As they had presumed Frederik to be one of the movers, it perceptibly triggered the thought in Bob's mind to allow them to believe that this was, in fact, the case. At the same time he realized he could more easily and less expensively pay Frederik to assist him rather, than as initially planned, to find someone to hire locally on a temporary basis for the day, a custom practiced by many small moving outfits in rural communities. This he shared with Frederik and was what they agreed to do.

Frederik enthusiastically seized the opportunity, having nowhere to go and sensed he had already begun a new life away from home with this first break. At the same time, in some way which he chose not to dwell on, he realized how uncertain this temporary job and new beginning was in reality, although as this was all he had at the moment, was at least something for him to grasp.

He began to work eagerly alongside Bob, learning, as he removed boxes and furniture from the van, how to correctly load the dolly, when not to try moving anything too large to handle on his own, and careful to not strain himself. It was a technique he knew he needed to swiftly acquire and with the sturdy wide belt Bob had loaned him to tightly wrap around his waist, he acquired what felt to be added strength.

Frederik was enthusiastic and found the Grayson's home the most beautiful place he had ever seen, realizing they had appeared to be aware of his reaction to it from the moment he had stepped inside the door. They were not only stirred by this, but were also sympathetic towards him while watching him work so earnestly, and seemed to like Frederik, who needed heartening.

Bob, at one point, before the completion of the job, had decided to share with the Graysons what he had learned in talking with Frederik while driving, despite having just met him. He took them aside, explaining Frederik's circumstances as he had understood them, and his having mentioned that he was hoping "he would never have to return" to what seemed to have been more than just an unhappy home and hopeless environment.

They worked until dark completing the move, at which time Frederik became painfully aware, as Bob was already mindful well before him, that he had nowhere to go. Just as they were pulling up the wide door at the back of the van, having loaded up the padding and dollies, Mrs. Grayson stepped outside and invited Frederik to stay and join them for supper which, without hesitancy, he enthusiastically and gratefully accepted. Bob whose work was done bade them goodbye and left to return home, feeling a small tinge of relief in having left Frederik with this outwardly considerate and thoughtful couple, hoping that only good would come of it. Frederik knew that he had been more than fortunate in meeting Bob as well as the Graysons.

At dinner after a somewhat wandering discussion, Frederik realized that the Graysons were trying not to appear overly inquisitive, but after a good hot meal and warm encouragement, he had been willing to talk about his circumstances with them. He spoke in only some detail about growing up, his life at home, and why he had appeared with the van driver as he had. It was decided then and there that he was to spend the night, and in the morning, Mr. Grayson would take him along with him to his office and attempt to figure out how he might be able to help Frederik, who clearly had left home for what appeared to be good reason. It was an impulsive decision and what seemed right. Frederik could not believe his good luck.

Elena had sat next to Frederik listening intently to his story, astounded to learn how much had taken place on the day he had left Elden, and urging him to continue. Frederik then continued to tell her about what then led to his new life during the five years that had passed.

Without much time to discuss or fully understand Frederik's unhappy situation, the Graysons decision to attempt to help him and to see if possible that he had an opportunity that could lead to a better life was instinctive. Frederik, if willing to work hard, could have a chance to improve his life, a remarkable gift. Their own grown children were gone now, living elsewhere, and they could make time for this. The Graysons were generous people. Frederik described sleeping that first night in a handsome four poster bed with crisp white sheets, cozy in the warm guest room of the Grayson's home, pinching himself to be certain it had not been just a dream. It was something he knew he would never forget. He felt more than elated. A lot had transpired in the years since this chance meeting.

Chapter 37

Things were not going well at Shangrila as bit by bit the news had slipped out that there had been a death there, although no details had, as yet, been given to the local paper, nor had anyone employed there disclosed this specifically to friends or neighbors, since those who knew only that it had, in fact, been a girl that died, just how had not been revealed to them. It had been Sgt. Reardon's strict order to the management to not inform employees or guests of the state of affairs and alarm them further, but to say merely the matter was being investigated.

The body had been discovered by one of the young girls who had gone back to the pool area after dark looking for the wet swimsuit bag she had carelessly left behind. It had not been clear to her whether the girl lying on the ground, whom she did not recognize, had fainted or slipped and fallen, and consequently did not find it particularly alarming, although she immediately ran to report it to a waitress in the small restaurant nearest by before hurrying to return to meet her friends for the bingo game that had already commenced in the game room, and for which prizes were to be given.

In an effort to determine which employees had been working on what shifts during that day and evening, it became clear that there had slowly developed a somewhat loose arrangement among the younger employees regarding their work schedules. While all posts needed to be covered and the work attended to, whether making up rooms at the Inn, waiting tables in the restaurants, maintenance jobs or whatever, employees had for some time been taking license in often switching their hours and positions to suit themselves, so that the schedules drafted each week in the office were unreliable as to who was doing what job and when.

The Manager had initially encouraged this form of rotation when new employees were hired in order to acquaint them with all aspects of work at Shangrila and prepare them to be ready to pitch in when and where needed. To his knowledge however, this routine of learning the various jobs ended once a more permanent position was assigned for most although there were some, such as Justin Faber and one or two others who were considered permanently unassigned and generally asked to fill in where needed when they came to work.

While focusing more on overseeing food supplies purchased for the main restaurant and two smaller ones, plus service to the guests, he had failed to notice the changes and switches in assignments the employees were making on their own, and was now distraught at not being able to provide Sgt. Reardon and Detective Branch with specific proof or details as to the whereabouts of all of the employees on that critical day. Drawing up a list of suspects was therefore more than a challenge while at the same time attempting to not reveal to the employees and guests that there had been a murder. This was not going to be an early night once again for Sgt. Reardon, who had planned to retire early and watch the baseball series that had just begun.

Reviewing the guest list of all who had been there that could or could not be accounted for, provided an additional dilemma for the investigation even though it had not been a particularly busy weekend at that time, with only a handful of families staying at the Inn and dining in the restaurants. Sgt. Reardon stressed to the Manager that someone must know what had happened, and they needed to find out who it was. Someone on the grounds at Shangrila had killed the girl, and for what reason? Was there anyone else involved?

Having met the Chandras not just on this occasion but stopping in the 7-Eleven for gas, coffee and sandwiches over the past few years while attending the Police Academy along with visits returning to Elden to visit his parents, Sgt. Reardon had struck up an acquaintance with them and felt particularly anxious to get to the bottom of the matter and find the killer. The Chandras were nice people to whom this should not have happened.

Chapter 38

Looking back, a lot had happened in the town of Victor after Mathew Reardon had first arrived. Once having made the decision to leave his parent's family farm in Elden and move to Victor to attend the Police Academy, the lives of others from Elden who also came were changed, as well as his own.

Growing up in the small town, he had collected news and stories about the Academy since he had first seen them in local ads and papers when only fourteen, and had saved them secretly in a box under his bed, knowing this was what he wanted to do once he was on his own. His father, a local farmer with a sizeable piece of land on which he grew crops of corn, wheat and barley, had taught his son all aspects of the business, expecting Mathew to continue working with him and eventually take over management of the farm when he, like so many others, would find it impossible to meet the demands and requirements of his farming business once age and infirmity advanced. His son however knew that he had been cut out for something else.

Mathew Reardon had been one of the first boys in town to have a car of his own and had used it to his advantage on more than one occasion, finding most of the local girls more than delighted to go for a ride with him outside the confines of Main Street. On one occasion he had finally driven to Victor, bursting with curiosity and desire to visit the Police Academy. Unfortunately it had already closed that day by the time he and Sharon Retton arrived late in the afternoon.

They had, nevertheless, lingered in town, finding a small, cozy restaurant nearby to have dinner, spent time together parked on the hill overlooking town, and driven back to Elden, arriving well after midnight. It was not their first date. Mathew had graduated from the Elden High School several years ahead of Sharon but had noticed her for months driving the new car her father had purchased for her sixteenth birthday before asking her to a movie. Mathew was not the only boy she had been seeing, although her continuous flirtations and associations with others generally served indirectly to kindle the flame of desire in those in whom she was most attracted.

Mathew was someone that more than interested her among others, and his preoccupation with attending the Police Academy and plan to leave town both annoyed and at the same time represented a challenge to her, one that she viewed as significant. It wasn't long before he acknowledged her fixation for him, no longer something she managed to conceal, or he ignore, and they began to see more and more of each other, always discreetly, in various places, spending hours together where they could be intimate. At the same time, Mathew had been spending more and more time focusing on his goal to leave the farm, anxious and concerned about his family's obsession with keeping him there to take over at some point. Mathew Reardon had, at that time, needed to make some decisions soon.

Chapter 39

Another person who had gone to Victor about the same time as Mathew Reardon, only for a very different purpose and under different circumstances, had been Sharon Retton's mother, Gloria. Noticing a small ad in the Help Wanted section of the local newspaper captioned: "Executive Hostess/Receptionist for a small growing company", she had cut it out, given some thought to it and finally called to schedule an interview. Once accomplished, she set out early one morning for the drive to Victor. This action represented a complex set of prerequisites for her, but the curiosity and appeal of some involvement in the business world outside of Elden at that point held its mystery and had proven to be fruitful.

Gloria arrived early the first day at her new job in Victor and parked her convertible across the street in full view of most of the windows on the third floor facing west. Everyone who had already arrived at work, filled their coffee mugs and were at their desks, strained to watch her step out of her car and walk towards the building. As her interview had taken place in the first floor conference room a week earlier, few of the employees other than Frank Grayson who had interviewed and hired her had seen her before. Gloria was an exceptionally attractive woman, with soft blond shoulder length hair and the same good figure she had when Bill Retton had first seen her. She still turned men's heads.

With the plan underway to entirely restructure and streamline the operation of the company, Frank Grayson who had been hired for this purpose, had also undertaken to redecorate all three floors of the building, including giving the façade a badly needed face lift. He had opined that in keeping with the new company image, having an attractive assistant to greet business associates and work with him would be a constructive and worthwhile addition, and had created and designed a small stylish reception room at the main entry which had just been completed. Gloria Retton had been the first to respond to his ad in the county newspaper and he had hired her instantaneously.

The newly decorated reception room just inside the front door, not more than ten by twelve feet, featured a modern silver toned grass-cloth wallpaper, a smart, sleek desk of stainless steel with two small drawers, just enough for a few pens, pads and small desk essentials to not disturb the handsome design, jet black upholstery with a subtle thin silver thread randomly running through on the seats of two contemporary steel arm chairs, a black and silver-grey striped settee with matching cushions, a small, modern chrome swivel desk chair and a bookcase of chrome and glass behind the desk. The floor had been carpeted with soft, grey, knotted wool and Grayson had particularly enjoyed selecting the artwork for the small gem of an office, in which he had taken great personal interest in decorating. In browsing at a local gallery, he had somewhat impulsively selected a large reproduction of an Andy Warhol silkscreen portrait of Marilyn Monroe to place as the final touch on the wall behind the settee.

The attention Frank Grayson had given to this space was a strident leap in decorating given that the factory-like atmosphere had, prior to his arrival, featured fluorescent lighting and linoleum floors unsuccessfully disguised as marble tiles by some factory engineer who had devotedly come up with the design. This had all been created more than forty years earlier when the building had been the home of an air conditioning plant, and there was plenty of work yet to be done.

While planned changes to the building had been put in motion although, as yet remained in the early stages, final touches to the entry, reception room and adjacent conference room had been completed earlier that week as Frank Grayson was well aware that the entry and first floor area would be the first impression for anyone visiting and at times, all that would be seen by their clients. Office, lab and workroom space on the second and third floors were not always visited by clients although the overall impression was important to him and he did not leave them out of his general overall plan for the pending makeover.

The upgrade and redecorating was also intended to improve morale, although with the company's more important streamlining and consequent added expense, there was some apprehension on the part of employees of the possibility of dismissal of some positions to follow. It had not as yet been made clear who might or might not benefit from the reorganization and employees had recently become noticeably more conscientious in arriving for work on time and not being the first out the door at closing time.

Frank Grayson was waiting for Gloria Retton downstairs near the front door after having already discreetly watched her cross the street below from his small office on the second floor. The employees who had been granted window seats also did not fail to enjoy watching her arrival. Here from this position he could also observe what might be some important elements of workroom procedures or better yet, matters that needed attention, in the adjacent open office space that could be in need of modification or possible elimination.

Gloria had worn a two-piece red suit which he noted to himself looked especially attractive as she sat down with him to discuss her new role, both having entered the reception office with its black, chrome and silver touches, and that her suit was coincidentally the color worn by Marilyn Monroe in the large reproduction Warhol silkscreen print he had, quite satisfyingly, selected and hung on the wall over the sofa. It also occurred to him that he could have confidence in her choice of attire to effectively complement the new look at the firm, as having now observed her smart and stylish appearance on two occasions, he had no doubt that she was the perfect image for them, She was introduced to all and shown around the entire firm before she sat down to read the details and plans about the company in her new office.

This job and the drive from her home in Elden, while a lengthy one, for now anyway, offered Gloria the getaway she was longing for. The silver-blue Ford convertible with cream colored interior leather seats and global positioning system was her vehicle to freedom from boredom. She had engaged Henry Jordan the day before her first day at work to thoroughly wash the outside and inside of her car and to apply two coats of wax with a final second buffing. Henry had spent the better part of the previous day, relishing every moment of this task, and had finally needed to be asked to complete it before he rubbed the paint off. Answering the ad had been the best thing she had done that month. Things were looking good to Gloria Retton.

Chapter 40

The situation at Shangrila had not improved and the Chandras had left the inn to go home, promising not to speak with the newspaper reporters who had begun to aggressively seek information from everyone they perceived to be connected, or to have visited there. Mr. Chandra's brother, Nelam's father, had not yet been notified but they knew it must be done immediately and were waiting for the clock to arrive at an hour appropriate for the call to New Delhi, another eleven hour delay. Knowing they had no explanation as yet for what had occurred, this was the worst call the Chandras had ever had to make.

Sgt. Mathew Reardon & Detective Kevin Branch had brought Sheriff Rodney Kastor to Shangrila again to meet with the Manager, the Assistant Manager and the few employees who knew more than others as they were making slow to little progress. It was becoming more and more evident that the incident would soon be broadcast to everyone, including to the papers, once someone decided to no longer withhold the story, at least as far as they felt they understood what had happened, and wanted to be the first to reveal it.

Sgt. Reardon would have liked to visit the Chandras, however, knew it was best not to in order to avoid gossip and suspicion that they were somehow involved although he thought constantly about them and of his promise to find the murderer. Before driving to the station each morning, he mentally reviewed the facts of the case as best he knew them, and all that had, and was, taking place. Not knowing where to begin again looking for new evidence continued to frustrate him.

When the body had discreetly been removed from Shangrila by Dr. Gregory and his workers from the Elden Clinic, the debate of what to do next had been a concern although neither any evidence such as fingerprints, blood or fluid samples, nor anything found near the body had provided any clues to work with. More importantly, Nelam's parents in India had as yet been notified. The Chandras were to give instructions as to what to do the next day after contacting them and it was likely that she would be cremated at the funeral home in Everton as this could not wait indefinitely.

The plan devised by Sheriff Rodney Kastor, Sgt. Mathew Reardon and Detective Kevin Branch was to first call on all of the guests who were staying there, hoping to obtain some clue or specific information as to something they may have seen or noticed, as well as any behavior on their part that might be considered suspicious. Their goal was to not alarm anyone but to leave no stone unturned in the event the murder had been committed by one of the guests. Although it seemed a difficult undertaking given that they could not discuss what had actually occurred, they knew it was important to do so before their vacations ended and they were scheduled to depart.

In addition, an interview was arranged with each employee, one by one, in an effort to determine who, according to the schedule, should have been working that day. Nothing was to be revealed to them, and they were to merely be asked what tasks they were assigned to or were performing that afternoon, and in what specific location. In this way, the team of officers and managers felt they could both establish who might be considered a suspect as well as to observe their behavior during the interview. Detective Branch claimed the interviews would reveal who was guilty and was as good as a lie detector. He felt certain that whoever had done it would have a hard time hiding his or her uneasiness and proudly named several incidences where he had nailed a guilty suspect using this interview technique. It seemed to the others that with no specific evidence it was a dubious manner of apprehending criminals although he was adamant that he would know. Sgt. Mathew Reardon kept his opinion on this method to himself as it did not concur with any interrogation techniques he had learned at the Police Academy.

It had been decided to conduct these interviews in the game room used for bingo and cards, and a kind of dais was set up for the group of five, Sheriff Rodney Kastor, Sgt. Mathew Reardon, Detective Kevin Branch, the Manager and his Assistant Manager, who would all ask the questions, either one at a time or overlapping one another to review and clarify the statements of each being questioned.

Calling in all the employees assigned to work that afternoon and evening meant that those who may not have been assigned officially that day to be there were exempt to some degree although they could presumably have switched positions with others which would remain undocumented. Some may have simply been on the grounds. Trying to pinpoint everyone's actions would be daunting, this was clear. Suspicion and gossip grew among many who worked there to an intensity that could soon burst and they feared for the reputation of Shangrila and their livelihoods, their biggest concern.

Chapter 41

Gloria Retton's new position at Tecto Associates in Victor had turned out to be just what she had hoped for. Leaving Elden each morning, having carefully selected what she would wear to work then sliding into her silver-blue convertible, she drove across town, exiting onto the road heading southeast for Victor, sometimes stopping at the 7-Eleven part way there to pick up a cup of coffee for the remaining miles. The Chandras had unfailingly always been there, opening up each day before seven a.m. with coffee and sandwiches ready for the early morning workers headed either northwest toward the resort or southeast toward Victor, over the border in the next county and to the towns beyond.

Once at the office, Gloria had found no trouble in getting to know the other employees, sharing lunch and coffee breaks with many until she became familiar with all and popular with most of them, and while a few resented her seemingly stress-free and comfortable position, newly designed office space and obvious favor with the boss, it soon became apparent that she was not only decoratively but capably representing the firm as a kind of in-house hostess, often being the first to meet prospective clients as they came in, and demonstrating a talent for engaging them in detailed discussions regarding their requirements and expectations. Frank Grayson had been very pleased with himself for having found and hired her and assured her that she could advance within the company as much as she wished, taking on responsibilities to the extent she felt she could handle. He was, in fact, clearly more than impressed with Gloria. His interest in her was also noticed by others.

Despite the distance, the drive each day to Victor seemed effortless as there was a tolerable amount of traffic that allowed Gloria time to focus on the fact that she felt a freedom and sense of self-worth that she had not before had an opportunity to enjoy. Feeling trapped by the circumstances of being a bank chairman's wife in a small town where there was little to do, she had felt that bringing Sharon into the world had not been an altogether fulfilling experience nor had it brought her and Bill any closer together than had the design, construction and eventual occupation of the huge impressive home he had built for her. She wondered if this new life, miles from her home and family, was what she may have needed more. This was a new experience to treat carefully and to make the most of and she knew it.

Chapter 42

The "interviews" with employees at Shangrila, as they had been discreetly termed, were going slowly as most of the guests there at the time of the incident had left and were in various stages of being contacted and interviewed. The employees who had mistakenly assumed their devious rearrangements of duty days and positions were the subject of why they were being questioned had complicated the matter further by attempting to disguise and tightly guard their having exchanged places with others and agreed with them to tell the same story. Consequently determining who was in fact working and where at the resort, having narrowed down the hours to between four and six-thirty the day of the murder to be a likely time for the incident to have taken place, revealed only a few possible suspects, with mostly all other employees engaged and witnessed at work in the restaurants, the inn or in other locations, at least according to their stories.

The guests who had been aware only that an ambulance had come and taken someone to the hospital, had considered it, for the most part, a matter of course in such a large resort and had not been aware that there had, in fact, been a death. None of those interviewed seemed a likely suspect in any sense as most were families who had been witnessed together on the tennis courts, dining at the inn or other restaurants or enjoying the pool area. Those that had been seen at the pool more than others were high on the list for possible second interviews once everyone had been contacted.

Chapter 43

A maintenance program had been established for the pool, the laundry, and the kitchens, the three locations where additional daily cleaning was necessary to meet the standards and requirements that allowed them to remain open. State Inspectors had paid an unexpected visit the year before to make a thorough investigation of how well the state mandates for running the resort were being observed, after several complaints and accusations had been made by disgruntled employees that had been let go.

The same inspections took place in the kitchens of the restaurants, the outside showers at the pool and tennis courts, bathrooms and wherever they deemed necessary to look. It was made clear in the report at the conclusion of their visit, that more attention needed to be made to the procedures in place for maintenance and that their team could, at any time, reappear for an unscheduled inspection.

Ted Horton, whose primary responsibility was maintenance of the pool and cabanas and who was in that location more than other employees, was questioned as to who had signed in and spent more time there and what he had noticed about them, if anything. He was interviewed by the inspection team's leader and asked to walk them through his routine for maintenance of the pool, and how often he was there.

Henry Jordan had been present the day of the state inspection and it had been noted that he seemed to be oddly and somewhat suspiciously inadequate as a qualified affiliate of the operating team at Shangrila. He shamelessly followed the team of inspectors as they went from building to building, drawing attention to himself and raising their suspicions as to his purpose in doing so.

Chapter 44

Three who had so far undisputedly been on duty that day, all called in to be interviewed, were nevertheless thought to be the most unlikely to have been responsible for the murder. The complexity of the matter lay in that any of the employees may not be telling the truth about exactly where they were and what they were doing and no one had been willing to specifically claim to notice where anyone else was among them.

Justin Faber, while considered a "floater" to go where needed when reporting for duty, had stated that he had arrived at three o'clock that day and had gone to finish the job begun the day before of checking the clocks and smoke alarms in each building to be certain they all had batteries and were in good working order. He had shown responsibility for the jobs assigned to him so far, and had not been one to engage in time swapping, proving to be reliable whenever called upon. He was ambitious and saving money to buy a car, which he spoke of incessantly, and was always anxious for holiday and overtime opportunities to be given to him as he worked toward this end. They all liked Justin and had spoken of a promotion for him before long. He appeared to be telling the truth and an up-front young man who had appeared to be grateful for his opportunity there. He was thanked and reminded, as all were, that he might be interviewed again at some point.

Ted had appeared to be nervous when questioned, his anxious demeanor and uneasiness noted. He seemed concerned that his job may be threatened, possibly by an unsatisfactory investigation, as he was solely responsible for both keeping the equipment in both satisfactory and safe operating condition, cleaning the pool and making certain the heating system was operational and at the correct temperature plus keeping the changing rooms clean and in good order. It was noted that his position at Shangrila had always been only part time as he worked there on days off from his postal responsibilities, along with holidays and weekends.

He had been known to flirt with the girls working at the resort, although his outgoing personality and social predisposition had earned him the reputation of being a pleasant and dependable employee. He would have been the most likely possible suspect due to the fact that he worked exclusively in the pool area although Detective Kevin Branch felt convinced after their interview with him that he was innocent of any wrong doing or of any specific knowledge other than possibly gossiping about what had happened. Kevin's theory of ferreting out a guilty or innocent person during just such a discussion appeared to his team a more than uncertain method and while all agreed Ted had shown responsibility for some years in working for the postal service in the county and dutifully sustained his position at Shangrila, still, little was known about him and he was in fact there at the time. Sgt. Mathew Reardon felt certain that he should be on the short list and wanted another discreet interview to be arranged.

Julian's father Alden Haber stated that he had not been at Shangrila that day, although he had been called earlier regarding a small plumbing issue at the inn which was not an emergency and which he had agreed to attend to when he could. Not being required to report specifically to anyone whenever he did go had been acceptable as he had a reliable record of repairing whatever needed attention and following up with detailed invoices for work completed. This had resulted in his being considered a reliable professional they could depend on for routine or emergency plumbing and electrical work. He was thought after the interview to be the least likely suspect.

Chapter 45

Karl Jenkins had been at Shangrila that day and had claimed he had made a visit for the purpose of making a proposal to handle the laundry and dry cleaning for guests staying at the Inn. The proposal was for all laundry to be picked up by his Laundry & Mending Company early mornings and delivered on a daily basis by four o'clock, thus eliminating the need for continuous repair and maintenance of the increasingly dated and unreliable laundry facilities on the grounds. He stated that he had met and spoken with the woman in charge of housekeeping at two o'clock and subsequently to the gentleman who appeared to be in charge of the laundry, located in a large bungalow to the rear of the inn. Guests could send laundry and dry cleaning with added rush service available anytime immediate attention was needed.

Karl stated that he had met a wiry, unpleasant little man by the name of Riley there who clearly did not want to lose his position if it was decided to close the in-house facility and award it to Mr. Jenkins' business, although he had been asked to show him around which he did begrudgingly. He mentioned that he had detected unusually nervous behavior and hastiness to end the meeting on Riley's part and mentioned this during his interview, suggesting that his own presence there was resented and considered a threat. This seemed to them an interesting comment worth further investigation and Sgt. Reardon made a note to add Riley to the list of those yet to be interviewed.

Initially unable to handle their volume of business when the inn had opened and once the restaurant had proven to be successful, Karl felt he now would be able to handle both his own business and that of the resort with his expanded facility. There had been problems at the inn at times with equipment breakdowns when he had been called upon to pick up, handle and return guest's laundry, and with his desire to permanently take over Shangrila's laundry business this was not the first time he had come with a proposal.

Because he had been on the property that afternoon, Sgt. Reardon had asked him to appear for a talk again a few days later with the panel of five in the game room at

Shangrila. Karl had hoped this second visit would mean they were considering him with regard to the possible attainment of a contract for the inn's business and nothing else. This represented a relief as well as a business prospect to him, and buoyed by the possibility it was that alone for which he was being interviewed, he carefully prepared himself, going over what he would say at the interview.

Chapter 46

One morning, not long after Gloria had begun to learn and use the company software, a new computer was delivered to her desk and by the following afternoon, installed and running. The previous week she had begun working with a local printing company, ordering stationery and business forms with the new company logo, purchase orders, business cards for all the technicians and officers, and had called on several manufacturers for quotes on a new sign. The decision was made to install a sturdy black canvas banner over the front door with the company name, Tecto Associates, in large white letters. This would replace the faded metal sign that had rusted and needed to be removed. She was working hard, gaining experience and noticeable admiration and approval from Frank Grayson, and she loved it. His admiration of Gloria was growing and it had been noticed by others.

Frank Grayson had come in later than usual one morning accompanied by a slender young man whom he introduced as Frederik, and asked Gloria to take him under her wing for the rest of the week, introducing him to the staff and officers, showing him around the firm, finding small jobs and errands he could do, plus assisting others as best possible with work in progress. She found him anxious to please and willing to plunge in with whatever small or large task he was given, and suggested to Frank Grayson that he might be a good candidate for a number of jobs but that he seemed to have had little or no experience, unspecified talents and needed training. That paradoxically made two of them, both having come to Tecto Associates with no background or experience in business, although Gloria had already quickly begun to gain her footing. Both, in their own way, had miles to go; it was a remarkable moment in time and opportunity for both Gloria and for Frederik. Things were looking good for both of them.

Chapter 47

About the same time that Gloria had become employed at Tecto, Mathew Reardon was completing his studies at the Police Academy in Victor, having realized that with his strong commitment and hard work he had been able to complete the program in a shorter time than first expected.

Given that he had needed to make his savings last to see him through the time he would spend at the Academy, he had proceeded to make this his goal, depriving himself of most leisure pursuits and time off, other than participation with his fellow classmates in weekend baseball games, and stopping at James' Tavern in town after the games for a beer and some comradery before getting back to his studies.

He had met and hit it off with a fellow classmate on his first day at the academy and they had agreed to share the small apartment he had found over a stationery store on the main street of Victor. As both were of the same mind to work hard and complete the courses in as short a time as possible, they had found it to be an ideal arrangement, while at the same time enabling Mathew to cut down on his costs. His father, while disappointed with Mathew's decision to leave the farm, had unexpectedly offered to pay a substantial portion of his expenses in support and Mathew had eagerly progressed toward his goal and worked hard to achieve it.

Chapter 48

Sharon Retton appeared unexpectedly one Saturday, and after inquiring around town and establishing where Mathew was living, was waiting for him when he returned. He had decided to skip having a celebratory beer with his teammates at the tavern that morning, despite the elation he felt at having just pitched the final winning game. He had however, needed to prepare for one of his final exams the following week and had headed straight home. He found her standing just inside the stationery store's front door where he couldn't miss seeing her, as the entrance to his apartment above was an adjacent doorway leading upstairs. It was eleven in the morning and the start of a day he had not planned for.

Sharon Retton was wearing a soft light grey colored v-neck cashmere sweater pulled smoothly over her breasts, a pair of tight darker grey slacks, her long blond hair pulled up into a chignon with a small silver clip, and a simple strand of pearls at her neck. She looked beautiful and much more sophisticated than she had the last time he had seen her and while for a moment he felt the rush of her presence and their once intimate relationship, struggled, searching for the right words, knowing he did not want a continued involvement with her now, just when he had focused on something that meant so much to him and had been a dream for so long.

They spoke awkwardly, as he hoped to not show disappointment in seeing her, fully aware that she had come intending to see him. Having recognized his reserve, Sharon quickly recovered and announced that she had in fact come to visit her Mother who was working in Victor and had unexpectedly been called in to work that Saturday. She then unpredictably and somewhat impulsively suggested to Mathew that he join them in an hour for lunch once he had freshened up, and promptly turned to leave, after telling him where to meet them.

Although startled by her unexpected visit, Mathew felt both relief and a touch of disappointment at the same time, knowing he was backing away from something he did not then have and yet may have wanted, a woman's companionship, a relationship. Deep inside however he knew that he did not want to again become involved with Sharon despite their past affair. He went upstairs, showered and prepared to meet Sharon and her mother for lunch, feeling he had somehow let her see that he was no longer interested in her although she had apparently acknowledged it and appeared to recover quickly, by casually inviting him to lunch. At that point, it seemed, in reality, to be a nice break for Mathew despite being a change in his plan to study, but feeling in control, he smiled in anticipation, confident knowing he could make up for his lost study time later in the day.

Chapter 49

Frederick having related the details of his meeting the van driver Bob and his meeting with the Grayson, had gone on to describe to Elena all they had done to help him get on his feet during the past five years. His enthusiasm was evident as he talked about the support they had shown him and he spoke unreservedly about how he had begun to receive training at Frank Grayson's company, Tecto Associates, his work part time there and attending college at their generous behest. He proudly told Elena about the degree in Business Management he was close to earning and that he would soon be working full time in the Technical Support Department at the company with good prospects for promotion. Both he and Elena had achieved a lot since leaving Elden and they enthusiastically shared their stories of the hard work, good luck and success they had both experienced.

Frederik also spoke more in detail about Frank Grayson, who, in moving Tecto Associates forward as he had successfully done, had been given stock options in the company and done exceedingly well. In addition, by investing in the initial stock options of several other large corporations engaged in the same technological pursuits and development as his own company, he had understood the infinite possibilities not as yet developed but at the cutting edge of new ideas, and had benefitted from his keen attention to what was most likely on the drawing boards. Frank closely observed ever newer ways of doing things as they continuously developed. Tecto Associates was doing well, as was Frank Grayson himself.

Frederik knew that Frank had been solely responsible for giving him the break he so badly needed and felt his life had turned around and was on a good solid track. There were, however, some disturbing issues and developments that were a serious concern to him.

Chapter 50

The lunch with Gloria Retton and her daughter Sharon had been for Matthew, a completely unanticipated and disorienting experience as it had begun to interfere with his studies and inhabit his thoughts from the moment they left the lunch room on Victor's Main Street. While Sharon had once been a preoccupation of his for some time when they had first met in Elden and begun their affair, his reaction to her mother Gloria, who was nineteen years older than Mathew, had an entirely different and more intense effect on him, and he was at a loss to comprehend the immediate and strong attraction he felt towards her.

The conversation at lunch centered primarily on Sharon, fundamentally initiated by her, as she chatted nonchalantly about her new job, her friends and activities, assuming the focus to be on herself, while unaware of the subtle but intense awareness of each other that Mathew and Gloria were experiencing across the table from one another. Mathew neither said much about his studies at the Police Academy and his current life nor did Gloria talk about her position at the company in Victor, however it was clear as they said goodbye and he felt the soft squeeze of her hand in his as they parted that he would be seeing her soon again.

Chapter 51

Sharon realized that the attractive young man who had caught her eye looked familiar as she had stepped inside the front door of Tecto Associates late that afternoon after lunch. She had come to say goodbye to her mother, intending to make it clear to Mathew in so doing that she had in fact not come to Victor to see him. Sharon asked to be introduced to Frederik who by then, had decreased the number of hours he spent at the company as he was enrolled at Hanover College and concentrating intensely on his classes, all at the suggestion, support and encouragement of Frank Grayson. He happened to be there that weekend to work on preliminary specifications in the technical department for a new computer system that was planned to upgrade what was currently in place in the company.

Frederik recognized her immediately, as he had assumed after meeting Gloria Retton, when Frank Grayson had introduced her the first morning he had arrived at Tecto, that he would no doubt eventually see her daughter Sharon. He had anticipated this day with mixed feelings and found himself to be surprisingly nervous as they shook hands. Sharon was as beautiful as he had remembered her to be when he had first developed a crush on her when only 16 back in school in Elden and despite the time that had passed, assuming she was probably still unapproachable, found himself nevertheless suggesting they have coffee together.

After having felt she had been somewhat disregarded and even more or less snubbed by Mathew Reardon, whom it was she had in fact actually driven to Victor to see, she replied agreeably that she would love to and sat in Gloria's office admiring the elegant, sleek, black, silver and chrome décor while waiting for Frederik to complete what he had been working on and join her.

She had at that point recognized who Frederik was, as her Mother had at one time mentioned to her that someone who had been in school with her at Elden High School was now working in her company. The fact that he had now significantly changed and become self-assured as well as an attractive young man interested her. This turn-of-events pleased Sharon and she could see that her day had not been a complete loss but had, in fact, taken an interesting diversion from its initial design. It had been a remarkable day for Gloria Retton, for Mathew Reardon and for both Frederik and Sharon.

Frank Grayson watched from the second floor window of his office as Frederik and Sharon walked across the street together toward the coffee shop around the corner and wondered at the same time who Gloria had met for lunch so mysteriously when she had in fact pledged to work that full day as she had been gone more than a couple of hours. He had for quite some time become more and more aware of a growing attraction to her and a realization of how well and closely they were working together to improve the image and volume of business for the company. He had also begun to depend on her in more ways than he wanted to admit to himself, disregarding the danger in allowing his attraction for her to continue. She was, after all, a married woman as he was himself, a married man. Perhaps it would be interesting to meet Bill Retton.

Chapter 52

The official news had finally broken in Elden that the death at Shangrila, which had by then been known of for some time although in not much detail, had the added intrigue of being possibly more than an accident or natural death and may have been a murder or suicide. Maintaining any strict control over the employees regarding the matter which they had been advised to not discuss with anyone, had proven impossible and with no real evidence, leads or witnesses the investigation had come to a standstill.

There had been no clear strategic plan to move ahead after guests who had been staying at the Inn at that time had been contacted and interviewed either by telephone or in person in the case of anyone who lived within driving distance. Sgt. Reardon and Detective Branch had been busy either driving to meet with the guests who were willing to meet either half way, or open the doors to them in their homes to be interviewed. All but one had been contacted and no progress made. They would need to drive to Victor to meet with the last guest who had, so far, not been reached for an interview appointment.

Detective Branch had one by one crossed off names on the list once they had met with them and determined they appeared not to be guilty of any knowledge or involvement in the death of the young girl. His added proclaimed skill of recognizing any guilty behavior when interviewing served well to cut these otherwise time consuming visits in half as he detected none during their meetings. He was very proud of this self-acclaimed attribute and didn't hesitate to continue speaking highly of himself with regard to it. Kevin Branch liked to be in control of things. This was an obvious feature of his personality.

The lack of success in finding a suspect among the few guests who were at the Inn, most of whom seemed unlikely candidates in the first place led them back to the decision to look again more closely at what may have been going on that dreadful day in the afternoon and just which ones could be narrowed down to have possibly been the murderer. Something had to happen and happen soon with this investigation.

After reviewing their pages of notes, going over the lists of employees and conferring with Sheriff Kastor and the Inn Manager who had been the primary representative of Shangrila during the investigation, a meeting was arranged to be set up in the small snack bar located just south of the pool for a more intense series of interviews with staff members.

They were to be called in for a closer look and an accompanied visit made one-by-one to the spot where the girl's body was found in order to have an opportunity to observe the reaction of each person when there and to possibly find their story to be in conflict with their first statements. With nothing else to go on, the snack bar was scheduled to be closed for the following few days so it could be used for this purpose. It was agreed that staff members were to be invited to sit down for an informal cup of coffee in order to create a relaxed atmosphere and have it appear as simply a follow up meeting before being led out to the scene of the crime.

A list was drawn up and the first interview was to begin with the waitress who first told of the girl lying outside and had been the one to report it. She had been overlooked initially as it did not appear that she had actually gone near the body although when the Manager could not be contacted immediately, it had been Riley from the laundry department that she had found to be unoccupied and asked to go to help the girl who had evidently fainted.

She had gone with him then and been the one who in fact had first realized that the girl was dead. The two of them, presumably never having seen a dead body as they both claimed, ran quickly to the front desk at the Inn where the young man on duty that evening had called to Sheriff Kastor's office, found him in, and reported there was a body beside the pool. Sgt. Reardon and Detective Branch had both been called immediately and had arrived at Shangrila within the next forty-five minutes, both coming from Hemmings where they had been asked to be present in the lobby of the Bank of Hemmings, where a large late afternoon reception was in progress. It had been decided that only the one bank Security Guard may not have been sufficient with such an unusually large crowd.

Chapter 53

Back when in Victor, despite his intended focus at that time on his studies at the Police Academy, seeing Gloria Retton again after their meeting at lunch with Sharon had become an obsession with Mathew Reardon and as she had experienced the same intense reaction to him, had made plans to go the following Saturday to Victor, not mentioning this to Frank Grayson nor planning to go to the office at all. She called the number of the Police Academy and left a message for Mathew to call her. This he did immediately when the note had been handed to him during his last class of the morning and with heart pounding he made the call.

When Gloria arrived around noon that Saturday in Victor, Mathew was waiting for her at the restaurant where they had first met and having no place to go after lunch, they unwisely went back to Gloria's front office at Tecto Associates, believing Frank Grayson to be out of town on business. They assumed it unlikely there would be more than one or two employees working that day upstairs in the laboratory which was behind a plaster wall in one of the inside offices, and they spent the afternoon making love on the sofa in her small office with the door firmly locked.

From then on they began to meet whenever possible at the end of the workday before Gloria began her drive back to Elden, and on weekends, often finding motels in the small communities between Elden and Vincent where they could be alone. To them there was no pretense or need to clarify to each other what these encounters represented or what might follow as their sexual attraction for one another had clearly been what brought them together and they reveled in the sexual pleasure they had found in one another, not concerning themselves with where it could lead.

Chapter 54

Frederik who had begun to handle some small projects at the office with Gloria, mostly relating to reorganization details initiated by Frank Grayson, had noticed that she had appeared to lose interest in projects they had earlier been enthusiastic about working on together and when he was at the office between classes was well aware that she was slipping away from work earlier and earlier with no explanation. He had made no comment to Frank Grayson, assuming he must have noticed her curious behavior as well, which indeed he had but had oddly not appeared to react to for whatever reason.

Chapter 55

One Saturday morning when Frederik had come in to work early at Tecto Associates after having been in classes most of the week, he was surprised when Sharon Retton had shown up unexpectedly, claiming she was there to see her mother and possibly have lunch with her. As Frederik had not seen Gloria, at least not yet that day, and had not expected her to come in, he was as puzzled as Sharon also appeared to be when he told her that she was not expected, nor there. Having then established that lunch with Gloria was apparently not going to take place since she had clearly not shown up, Sharon suggested that instead they step out together for a bite to eat. While this meant leaving behind work that he had purposely come in to do, Frederik nevertheless succumbed to her suggestion, not unhappy to be in Sharon's company, and locking the door to the office, they began walking across the street. They walked slowly, discussing the weather, where Gloria might be, and headed around the corner toward the restaurant where Sharon had not that long ago invited Mathew to join her and her mother for lunch.

Sharon's real reason for going to Victor that day had in fact quite purposefully been to see Frederik whom she had found both charming and appealing, especially after having realized that he had been the young man she had wanted to attract years earlier when both were in high school, but had failed to do.

As Gloria had in fact mentioned casually that morning at breakfast to her husband Bill, with Sharon still present at the table, that she was going to be working at the office in Victor on a special project that day, it had provided the perfect excuse for Sharon to also drive to the office and drop in, knowing that as Frederik was finishing up courses at college, he by then tended to work on weekends at the company. Not finding her mother there at the office when she had arrived was not immediately a concern of Sharon's, given that it was not her intended purpose for going anyway although she did wonder why in fact her mother was not in the office.

In keeping with her fundamental need to override anyone's possible lack of interest in her and to instead develop a different response of admiration and awe, something which she had become accustomed to, she was determined to set about making this happen with Frederik, her motivation and impulse at least for the time being. Sharon was very much in focus, having thought a lot about Mathew Reardon's coolness toward her and was reacting accordingly.

Frederik, thinking to himself it odd that Sharon had been under the impression that her mother would be at work that day when she had in fact not been there on any other Saturday after the first few times she had come in when work was pressing, and even then, without a word, had slipped away for an extended lunch break when they were in the midst of a planned project, did not directly question Sharon about it although her visit did seem curious to him.

He also noticed that she showed a familiarity towards him that he was unaccustomed to and which led him to believe there was some ulterior motive she had concealed from him when showing up as she had. There was no question that he had been attracted to her long ago and again now that she had reappeared in his life, although he was uncertain as to just why it had come about and where it could possibly lead. Frederik thought to himself that he needed, for some reason, to be cautious about developing a friendship with Sharon.

Knowing that Mathew had often frequented the tavern with his friends where they were now headed gave Sharon the added pleasure of thinking he might be there to see her walking in with someone else after having, not so subtly, made her aware on her last visit that he was no longer interested in her. Sharon was not accustomed to being snubbed or disregarded.

Chapter 56

They arrived at the door to the restaurant just as a group of boisterous young men, possibly students at the Police Academy were leaving. Entering together they asked the waitress who greeted them for a table for two. Approaching the recently vacated table they were being led to near a window, they were stunned as they simultaneously spotted them sitting together in a booth at the opposite side of the room. Unaware just how either of their immediate reaction was affecting the other or for that matter themselves at seeing Gloria and Mathew together, they sat down, both feeling dazed, wondering how to interpret what they had just seen and not knowing what to say. This was a scene Sharon had not expected nor wanted to see, Mathew with another woman, let alone her own mother, nor could Frederik believe that Gloria who was clearly not in town to work, would have driven all this way on a day off to meet Mathew Reardon whom he knew to be in Victor studying at the Police Academy. He had run in to him in town several times and had remembered having seen him often in Elden years back when he was several years ahead of him in school.

Gloria and Mathew had not as yet turned to look across the room to discover them and see the dumbfounded look on their faces. With no clear plan quickly surfacing in either of their minds, and not knowing whether to get up and leave the restaurant quickly before being spotted or to wait and be discovered themselves, or to confront them, Frederik and Sharon both sat, woodenly staring at the menu, frozen in silence and shock. It was a moment none of them would forget.

Chapter 57

Ted had completed his last rounds of the day and headed to Shangrila where he often stopped in after his postal rounds to have a drink at the bar at the Inn and chat with others if not obligated to attend to any maintenance. There were often employees on their day off sitting at the bar along with some of the guests, and this proved often to be an opportunity to meet someone new as well as to pick up on the local gossip and at this particular time, any news of the investigation going on. He sat down, ordered a beer and attempted to strike up a conversation with the waitress next to him, who, also having just completed work on her shift, was enjoying a drink before leaving to go home.

The topic of conversation among most of the employees was now the murder, which rumor had supported, and although all of them had been cautioned to not discuss it, particularly at the bar where guests could overhear them, Ted urged the waitress he had seated himself beside to tell him what she had heard and if there had been anything new that she had learned about the investigation. He was anxious to hear what she had to say although realized he could not press too hard for details lest she become suspicious. He was not the only one wondering just how much had been discovered.

As the case was now becoming common knowledge to all at Shangrila, it had become impossible to keep the story completely away from the town folks and the local paper had tentatively alluded to the matter although under pressure from Sheriff Kastor had not yet printed a specific story as it was still under investigation with no person as yet identified as being responsible.

The death, now rumored widely to be, in fact, a murder, was the biggest news in town and the surrounding communities in many years and was a scandalous explosive waiting to burst. The owners and managers at Shangrila were holding their breath knowing the devastating damage this news would cause to their business and the pressure was mounting to find the killer. Sgt, Reardon had been present at every interview and cross examination but with no forensic evidence and inaccurate records of employee's whereabouts that day, he was hoping that the focus on the few most likely would reveal what they needed to learn.

With only one person from out of town who had been registered at the Inn the night of the murder to yet be questioned, and given that there was no evidence of any kind or apparent reason for the girl to have been killed, Reardon, Branch and Kastor along with the Manager and his Assistant Manager had no choice but to re-examine all of the employees and flush out who may not have been telling the truth, and better yet, might provide an answer to the gripping question that all were asking. They were yet to get an appointment to speak with the guest from Victor who had registered at Shangrila just before the murder but were planning a visit there, hopeful to check this last person of interest off their list as they had after meeting with other guests, and before proceeding to revisit all the staff members.

Chapter 58

Mathew had been the first to spot Frederik and Sharon sitting in the booth across the room, and was instantly shaken by the reality of how foolish he had been not only in allowing himself to become involved as he had with Gloria but to have jeopardized a lot more, including his impending graduation from the Police Academy. They had, since meeting, met often with abandon and now, hit with the undeniable awareness of what they had done, disregarding the fact that Gloria was not only a married woman but also the wife of a bank president, knew there could undoubtedly be more suffering for her than for him if their affair were to become known. A whirlwind of thoughts and realizations rushed frantically through his mind. He sat in silence for a moment, astounded at not just seeing Sharon there and with someone else, but for her to see him with her mother. Contemplating his next move and how to exit the restaurant without a scene he knew the situation could not have been worse for any of the four of them when in walked Frank Grayson who stood at the doorway for a moment before recognizing that it was Gloria with Mathew across the room that he was at that moment seeing. Having come in purposely to speak to Frederik whom he had just seen entering the restaurant while parking his car, he now made up the fifth in this circle of speechless individuals, all of whom felt suddenly caught in an inexplicable web.

Gloria who was sitting on the inside of the booth and absorbed with administering milk to the tasteless coffee she had been served, did not immediately turn to see the quiet pageant unfolding in the restaurant in which she was a participant, but noted that Mathew had suddenly become silent and had not responded to her comments. By the time she turned to witness the others, who now, at Frederik's suggestion, had risen and begun to head quickly toward Frank Grayson, still standing at the entrance, it was too late to pretend or imagine they had not been seen. Her stunned reaction saddened her intensely as it was all too suddenly clear that what had just occurred would end what had been the combination of not only the immense and once ripe abandoned pleasure in her relationship with Mathew but also, most likely, her position at Tecto Associates, and probably more disgrace to follow. This had been a very bad day for all of them.

Chapter 59

The Chandras had continued to put pressure on the Police Department for answers. The murder was discussed by all of their customers stopping in more often than ever by then at the 7-Eleven and many who by now had wondered if the murdered girl everyone was now talking about had anything to do with the Chandra's. Their distress, change in disposition and behavior had led them to put two and two together. The Chandras had spoken joyfully to so many customers of their niece's approaching visit prior to her arrival, all which stopped abruptly after their visit to Shangrila, and their sympathizers, assuming it was she who had been killed, joined with others, questioning why the killer was not being brought to justice.

Rumors flew among the staff and no one was assumed to be innocent, particularly Ted who many believed was the most likely to have been the murderer in that his job placed him working at the pool, the scene of the crime, and that he had a reputation for being flirtatious, and often seen watching the girls who gathered at the pool. In addition, very little was known about him, including where he lived, if he was married and how long he had been in the area. No one voiced this opinion openly although it was on the minds of many including Sgt. Reardon who disagreed with Detective Branch's doubtful assessment of innocence based on his interview with him.

Chapter 60

Exiting the restaurant, leaving Mathew Reardon and Gloria Retton still sitting in the booth in somewhat a state of shock, both uncertain how to proceed, Frederik had taken Sharon and Frank each firmly by the arm and led them to the parking lot where Frank broke away and walked quickly to his car before any words could be spoken. His interpretation of what he had just seen was something Frederik was certain Frank would either grasp as a threat or not immediately comprehend and that he might also be in some denial. Sharon stood motionless, with no apparent thought of what step to take next, while Frederik wondered if he shouldn't run after Frank before he started up the engine to drive off.

The scene ended there with Sharon then heading intently across the parking lot to her car to contemplate what she had just witnessed, and Frank speeding out of the lot in the opposite direction and away from Tecto Associates. Frederik slowly walked back to the office to collect his things. Mathew and Gloria had not as yet stepped out of the restaurant.

Chapter 61

The Chandras and Mr. Sharma who had begun to consider looking for a buyer and closing the 7-Eleven and Mechanics Shop, had been promised an answer to settle their family's despair which had not been forthcoming, and it had begun to appear that it might never come. Going back to India was not possible for either of them after the tragedy that had befallen them and beginning again in a new town seemed their only release from suffering and depression. Life could never again be for them the same although they had, through determination, saving and hard work been able to open their business in America and they were prepared to begin again if they had to.

Their hopes and dreams had been shattered and while only some of their regular customers had surmised that their sadness was related to the death everyone talked about at Shangrila, they had refused to comment to anyone and had carried on bravely, leaving still the question unanswered as to what had really happened there.

Chapter 62

Not long before, while installing new software in Frank's computer, Frederik had discovered a number of passionate, ardent letters written to Gloria but apparently never printed out nor delivered. It had been clear to Frederik for some time prior to this discovery that Frank was besotted with Gloria and he had contemplated approaching him with advice and warning to not persist. Frank had already indicated to him earlier that he had "great plans" for Gloria and it had become clear that he meant not just a promotion within the company. He saw that what lay ahead was a dangerous path for Frank Grayson.

Life for Frank had been good as his early success leading to the position as head of Tecto Associates had been far more rewarding than he had ever expected. His children were grown, successful on their own and he was soaring to even greater accomplishment and financial reward with a beautiful woman at his side in the company. He had carefully constructed in his mind that there could be a way to make Gloria a permanent part of his life. He was, in more than one respect, out of control.

Frank Grayson was not considering in his imaginings that he had a faithful and supportive wife of more than 30 years who had stood by him as they struggled in the early years of their marriage to raise their two children, finish college himself, and begin on the lower rung of the ladder to build a business career which had led to his current success. In addition, Frank was considered an upstanding member of the community, was on the Board of the Hospital and the Fire Department in Victor and had responsibilities to many including to Frederik whom he had taken in as though an adopted son and created a path for him to learn the business while getting an education as well as having recently confided in him as though he were in fact a son.

This confidence was an error he had blindly made as was his assumption that Gloria Retton seemingly and presumably had the same feelings toward him and would welcome his advances and schemes to include her in his realm. His daydreams and interpretations of them had led him beyond the reality of the world around him and he did not consider turning back.

Chapter 63

Sharon Retton had decided it was time for a change after her encounter in the restaurant, seeing Mathew and her mother together, and found that her father, Bill Retton, seemed to have arrived at the same conclusion as he came home one evening after a long day at the bank, and let her know that he felt "the entire family needed some changes". He suggested in no uncertain terms that she needed to look for a place of her own and that he was planning to put their house on the market for sale. As abrupt a decision as this seemed to Sharon who had been completely absorbed with her own life and requirements, it was uncannily the opportunity for change and the push she had needed to move on from what had become an unsatisfactory pursuit of anything and nothing and she all but welcomed it as her rescue.

Seeing her mother now for the first time in a role she perceived to be somewhat of a rival and having established no close or affectionate relations over the years with her, this seemed to represent the right move at the right time for her and probably for all of them. Bill Retton had worked hard to create a home for his wife and daughter but had recurrently begun to see their disappointments in feeling confined to their lives in a small town and how they had all grown apart from one another. He was tired and no longer felt obliged to maintain what had become a pretense to himself, to his family and to the town.

Chapter 64

Frederik knew that Frank Grayson had investigated financing with some of the regional banks when he had first come to Victor to begin planning the massive reorganization and redecoration of Tecto Associates. As Frederik's earnestness and hard work were more and more evident, Frank had shared his ideas and aspirations with Frederik and planned to involve him in the future in various areas of their expansion. One that had interested him as they discussed the structuring of a loan that had also offered an appealing low-interest package, was a small bank in Hemmings. Once Gloria Retton had begun to work at the firm and Frank had begun to find it difficult to avoid a growing and intense awareness of her, it dawned on him one morning when reviewing materials collected from several banks, that he had, in fact, met Bill Retton, Gloria's husband some time ago.

Another coincidence that took place shortly thereafter was when an invitation to a special reception for friends and clients of The Bank of Hemmings arrived in the mail addressed to him. He sat studying it for a long time before deciding that he wanted to see and meet Bill Retton again, but not to discuss the business of Tecto Associates or the possibility of financing a loan to the company. This was to be an entirely different encounter and Frederik noted that Frank began to speak about it often and fantasize how he would approach Bill Retton, and what he would say or do.

He had allowed himself to imagine that he could somehow have Gloria for himself and this obsession had begun to occupy his thoughts for so long, spiraling out of control, that the relationship he had in his mind with her had eventually grown to surpass the reality of their actual business connection which, to her, was just that, a workplace association which she was grateful and appreciative to have found. Her appeal, good looks and successful participation in the business that meant so much to Frank in this new business venture had overtaken his common sense although on the surface it was something he had believed he had successfully managed to conceal. This was a private matter that he wanted to resolve. Frederik became deeply concerned over what he had witnessed and heard.

Chapter 65

Cecily Watson in desperation to find someone to share her anguish, having heard nothing from Justin, had confided to her younger sister that she was pregnant and made her promise to not tell their parents. This she promptly did, seeing no reason to keep such a sensational piece of information to herself, assuring herself that she was revealing this important fact for Cecily's own good. This revelation to first her mother and subsequently to her father who gave no indication of possibly having been advised by their mother of the fact, led not only to Cecily being asked to leave the house due to the shame she was casting on the entire family, but to alienation from her mother who had chosen not to tell their father for fear of his reaction which was just what occurred, his asking Cecily to not set foot in the house again.

As Justin who had chosen to say nothing to his parents or to anyone else, had kept to himself and not called or attempted to see Cecily since her awkward disclosure to him of her condition, she had begun to write letters to him, posting them regularly and begging him to contact her and tell her that he loved her and would be there to stand beside her. As each letter she wrote had an increasing tone of desperation, and he had remained silent, she had felt more and more powerless and considered going to his house to confront him although she feared his possible rejection and chose not to appear there, at least for the time being.

With no choice but to put as many clothes and personal items together as she could manage, she knew she must quickly look for someplace to go as her father had demanded that she not be there when he returned from work the next day. Cecily called a friend in her office, a small insurance firm, who had recently rented a small apartment and mentioned that there was another apartment adjacent to hers that might still be available. Her job after graduation had paid little but she had saved her earnings while living at home hoping to create a nest egg for future use when needed and the time had now come when it was needed more than it would ever be.

She called and made arrangements to meet the manager who identified himself as Jake, praying the apartment would be not only affordable but immediately available. Fortunately it turned out to be both and by 5:00 pm that afternoon she had made a deposit, paid the first month's rent, been given the key and was able to move her few things into the small one bedroom apartment.

The former tenant who in fact had been a family member of one of the owners, had left a small but useful folding table, a few chairs, a decorative lamp and some dishes in the small galley kitchen along with a single bed which appeared to have been purchased recently and she realized how fortunate she was to not have to find these essential pieces with no time or much money to do so. She would keep her suitcases open on the floor to act as drawers until she could find something more suitable and just make do. At the end of that long day Cecily flopped down on the bed and as she began to fall soundly asleep, felt she never wanted to wake up to have to face so much uncertainty and doubt.

Chapter 66

Sharon Retton had begun the task of emptying her stuffed closets, packing shoes into boxes, her collection of handbags and totes, drawers filled with belts, jewelry and personal things, sweaters, jackets and all the trendy articles of clothing she had been unable to pass up as each new stylish fad had become popular over time. Realizing how much she had collected, at the same time taking for granted the beautiful room she had been accustomed to at home in which to accumulate, store and display what interested her at any given time, she felt a twinge of apprehension knowing she would miss the comforts of this luxury and living at home.

Hoping this would become something she could eventually forget, at the same time she was intrigued and excited at the prospect of change and what may lie ahead for her. Sharon guessed that she could probably stay temporarily for at least a few days with her friend who had recently moved away from her family's home in Elden to an apartment or better yet with Cecily Watson who was younger than she but a new friend whom she had recently met at the pool at Shangrila who had just mentioned to her that she was moving into the same two-unit building, suggesting she would be glad for a roommate to share costs. This would give her time to plan her move out of Elden to begin a new life, leaving behind Mathew, Frederik who lived in Victor, and who had also not shown adequate attentiveness to her as well as all the other boys in town, none of whom had measured up to her standards of essential requirements to receive her full attention. Mathew had been the only one that had fascinated and stirred her and now was the one person she hoped never to see again. Now that he was back in Elden working at the Police Department she knew that she could not stay. She placed a call to Cecily Watson and left her message.

Chapter 67

The experience at the restaurant in Victor, now some time back, had remained fresh in Mathew Reardon's mind as he had moved on to his job as Sgt. at the Police Department in Elden after graduation. He had learned the importance of considering possible consequences before carrying out his own selfish behavior and actions. He and Gloria had said their goodbyes then and there as both realized they had risked all that was at that time important to each of them, hurt people close to them as well as damaging their own future lives.

It was in some ways an easy parting despite the passion that had existed so intensely between them up to that moment, evidence of how quickly emotions can and do change. They made no plans to meet again. Both had uncertain days ahead of them that they would need to cope with and could only hope that they would be able to move on with no melodramatic or more serious consequences stemming from their relationship and affair. It had not been a happy ending between Gloria and Mathew but was behind them both now.

Chapter 68

The reception at The Bank of Hemmings was just far enough away and late enough in the day, that Frank Grayson had decided he would spend the day before and the night after the reception at Shangrila which he had heard so much about and he proceeded to call ahead and book a room for himself, explaining to his wife that he would be attending to business out of town, but not revealing his plan to indulge himself with a visit to Shangrila. He had wanted this time to be away and think about what lay ahead for him as he had a lot to consider. Life had become complex for Frank Grayson - he had made it so for himself. Frederik had been witness to this behavior and was aware of the trip Frank was planning in order to meet Bill Retton. He was clearly worried about Frank as he had shown great emotion in speaking about the matter.

It was difficult for Frederik to understand the relationships and the disappointing aftermaths among the people he had come to know and worked with. He had felt somewhat let down himself by their entanglements that had led only to unhappiness affecting all of them including his own growing sense of well-being. His supporter and mentor, Frank Grayson, had in some way revealed an undercurrent of selfishness in what had seemed an ideal world in which he lived. Frederik, having escaped from the unhappy drama of his own home life was finding himself unable to fully understand the behavior of those around him who seemingly had so much. He had witnessed a lot and was concerned about what might transpire.

Chapter 69

Frank Grayson had checked into his room at Shangrila, noting there was not a huge crowd at the dinner tables and realizing he could therefore enjoy a nice quiet swim after dinner before sunset in the beautiful pool he had discovered on his walk around the grounds. He was looking forward with both anxiety and trepidation to going to the reception the following evening at the bank in Hemmings and unsure of what his reaction would be or what he might say when meeting Bill Retton again after so much time had elapsed and since he had become infatuated with Bill's wife Gloria.

He vowed to himself he would remain in control and not act impulsively although his reckless abandon of reality was of little help to him. The decision to check in a day early had been a good one as he needed time to think and compose himself. He had something in mind but was uncertain just how he would handle it and how it might go. Frank Grayson was no longer in control of himself and the level headed, thinking and sensible person he had been not that long ago.

By then, oblivious to having seen Gloria with the younger Mathew Reardon in the restaurant, and refusing to acknowledge that it had been anything threatening to him personally or to his preconceived future plans for Gloria, Frank had laid out his suit that afternoon, polished his shoes and taken a nap before getting ready to drive to Hemmings to attend the bank reception. His overnight in Shangrila had been an unusual experience, much to his liking and had been satisfying in a number of unexpected ways so that he had begun to feel quite relaxed. He was at this point no longer himself in more than one way. By the time he awoke however he realized that not knowing the exact amount of time needed to drive to Hemmings, he may have overslept. He hurriedly showered and dressed, and although normally austere in appearance, put on a bright red and blue patterned tie and left the inn to drive down from the hills to the main road in Elden and on southwest on Route 3 to Hemmings to find the bank.

Chapter 70

Frank Grayson encountered unexpected traffic that late afternoon, people he assumed were probably leaving work early or beginning weekend trips, many possibly driving to Shangrila for the weekend, passing him in the opposite direction. He had passed one car in particular racing by, clearly exceeding the speed limit and appearing to endanger others on the road in their haste to get to whatever urgency had beckoned them.

It was already nearly 4:45 p.m. when he finally arrived in the parking lot of the bank, having inadvertently passed it once as it was on the opposite side of the road, requiring a turn-around in busy traffic. He parked the car, musing that arriving later than 4:00 p.m., given that the invitation had indicated 4:00 to 6:00 p.m. could somehow be to his advantage when encountering Bill Retton who would hopefully not be so preoccupied by that time with shaking hands and greeting guests, as most by then would have presumably arrived. He walked to the front door of the bank, adjusted his tie, and entered, to be greeted immediately by a hostess with a tray of a choice of Champagne or Perrier and quickly scanned the room wondering where in the sea of faces was Bill Retton.

To his surprise, Gloria who had been chatting near the doorway with a somewhat unusual looking, middle aged gentleman, dressed in what Frank disapprovingly considered an inappropriate outfit for a reception, that being a red blazer and jeans with an open shirt and no tie, spotted him, ended her conversation and moved across the room to his side. Glad to see her he was astonished when she asked what he was doing there, showing no evidence whatsoever of being glad to see him or even delighted that he had come. Considering his inability to realistically interpret anything she said to him as being possible disinterest or even negative, he assumed her to be behaving in this formal manner given that her husband was nearby somewhere in the crowd and fearful that he may be suspicious of their relationship.

Frank had for some time by then projected his own desires upon Gloria and had existed with the assumption that she must want what he did, while meticulously maintaining the businesslike pose she had at all times exhibited as they worked together in the presence of others in their work environment. The occasional lunches or drinks together outside of the office, generally which he himself had maneuvered in order to "discuss business", had led only to increase his longing for her while to her it had been a business relationship of mutual benefit only. He squeezed her hand and moved slowly into the crowd, tightly gripping the glass of champagne he had selected from the tray to the point of nearly snapping the stem as he turned from one face to the other in search of Bill Retton.

Chapter 71

Frederik had unexpectedly called Elena one afternoon asking her to join him in a trip back to Elden the next day to which she agreed, anxious to learn what was clearly concerning her brother. They met at the airport in Everton where Frederik was waiting for her at the landing gate and they proceeded to head north toward Hemmings, stopping to talk and have a late lunch in one of the many new restaurants that had sprung up along the road since they had left the area. They found a newer chain restaurant resembling an old coach house and were pleasantly surprised to be seated in a comfortable new faux red leather booth in a quiet and cozy beamed section of the restaurant, opposite a handsome long bar at the end of the room where a few young couples stood talking and sipping beer.

They talked for nearly an hour and Frederik explained his concerns about Frank Grayson, his trip to the Bank at Hemmings and his own apparent reasons for wanting to go as well. Elena could only agree that given his concern Frederik may as well go to the reception and hopefully not be sorry later that he had interfered. His concern for Frank Grayson and what he may be intending may have begun to become more of a concern than necessary, but Elena respected his loyalty and wanting to prevent, if possible, a tragedy which he had assumed could be in the making. She wondered if, while focusing so much on this, there could be another reason for Frederik's hasty desire to get back.

When they left the restaurant and continued on, Frederik planned to go directly to the bank in Hemmings. Whatever he felt he could do, if anything, to intercept or divert any undesirable action on Frank Grayson's part, was uncertain, although he was determined to go and try, hoping he might be able to stop anything from happening that could be devastating to everyone concerned. He dropped Elena off at the closest shopping mall to the bank, promising to return before it closed once it was determined where to meet, and Frederik continued on to make his visit to the bank. Elena had been glad he wanted to consult and share these concerns with her, wondering how the hours ahead would turn out and if there could be deeper meaning behind what she had learned and the real purpose for this visit.

Chapter 72

The Reception was still in full swing when Frederik arrived late in the day and found no one questioning whether he had an invitation as he entered the front door of the bank. It was a large impressive and stately building dating back to the 1930's and the high ceilings and grand pilasters around the walls made it seem the ideal place in which to entertain guests rather than to merely conduct dreary banking business.

Upon entering, he saw no sign of the Security Guard who had, in fact, been left alone on duty by that time and was not near the front door, but discreetly moving about the room in order to occasionally enjoy a sip of the champagne when not being observed. With those who had opted to enjoy the free champagne over the Perrier having already had more than one or two, the din of voices competing for attention and the crowd which had grown with a large number of guests arriving late, as he had himself, many coming after work or others from some distance away, it was clear that the pronounced 6:00 p.m. ending to the party had little chance of being observed as the appointed hour was likely to slip by, unnoticed by most.

Frederik who had no idea what Bill Retton might look like, began searching the crowd for Gloria and for Frank, hoping to dissuade him from initiating any trouble or doing anything foolish. As he was convinced that Frank had in mind to have some kind of a showdown with Bill Retton despite the ridiculousness of choosing that time and place to do so, his quiet observations of Frank's behavior during the past few weeks and overhearing his phone call to the bank stating in a strident manner that he "would be there and that they would know it" were enough of an indication to Frederik that he should step in and try to subdue Frank from what could be unfortunate and regrettable actions.

Frank Grayson had stepped into his life in a chance occurrence at a time when Frederik had no one to go to bat for him and offered much more than a helping hand

and support that led to his getting on his feet and creating a life for himself. It had been something he could not possibly have expected and for this reason, regardless of how irrationally and unreasonably Frank was now behaving, he cared for him as would a son or good friend, and wanted to be there for him.

Chapter 73

Sensing that Frank seemed troubled and angry, Gloria had suggested they step away from the crowded room to the outer wing of the bank that had been cleared of desks for the occasion as the beautiful tall windows on the west side of the building were one of the best features in the handsome old bank and needed to be featured for such an event rather than closed off. While only a few had moved into the high ceilinged wing, seeing as the bar where the champagne was being poured was located at the opposite side of the bank to the side of the tellers windows, it appeared at first to be empty and Frederik, not looking around the corner into the room, continued to push through the crowded bank lobby in search of either one of them.

Glad for Gloria's responsiveness to him in leading him aside, Frank's initial purpose in coming to meet Bill Retton was momentarily sidetracked as he was glad to have her full attention and to be nearly alone with her, dazed as always by her beauty and style. She looked particularly attractive this evening and Frank pictured her in the same silk dress at his side at one of their own future receptions or events. They had not been in the outer wing for more than five minutes when Bill Retton, who had not been the only one looking for his wife that evening, stepped into the room.

For some time his wife's departure every day and return to their home later and later each night as time went on had been a more than clear indication to him that she could no longer be trusted. It had taken some time for him to accept this as he had been unwilling and reluctant to face what he had deduced, once her absences, interest in him, her home and their daughter had diminished to the point it had, but was now ready to face it and to face her.

This was however not the occasion for either Bill Retton or Frank Grayson to settle either of their concerns with regard to Gloria and despite the tension that grew between all present as they stood stiffly observing one another, surprisingly not a word was said. The silence seemed to say volumes as each, concealing their own personal feelings, revealed nothing and everything.

Frederik, having covered all corners of the main floor in search of any or all of them with no luck, entered the wing at that moment where they all stood. Bill Retton without hesitation turned and as host of the reception, and ever a gentleman, courteously offered his hand to Frederik, introducing himself and asking if he would care for a glass of champagne as Frederik had no glass and had awkwardly approached them noting their silent stance. Unaware whom he might be, nothing else to Bill seemed worth saying at that moment as he had assumed the person speaking with his wife might in fact be a lover and was not about to create a scene at his own important gathering. Whatever needed to be said would have to wait until later and with an icy glance at his wife, he left the room. The reaction from Bill Retton to his wife provoked the reverse feeling in Frank from the attitude he had entered with, and he silently decided to himself that no confrontation would be suitable at that time for some unexplainable reason.

Gloria asked to be excused and made her way quickly out of the room and out of the bank sensing the encounter to be odd, troubling and disturbing. Frank inquired of Frederik as to his surprising presence there at the reception to which Frederik could only sheepishly stumble on the implausible excuse that he was on his way to his old home town in Elden for a few days and had remembered that Frank had mentioned he would be there.

Bill Retton, seeing that it was going on 7:00 p.m. began to conspicuously say goodnight to a few of the guests, which subtly encouraged others to take note of the time and begin to make appropriate gestures of departure. He was anxious for the evening to be over and to go home and have more than one drink, hoping that Gloria would in fact not be there that night. Things had changed for all of them at that point although it was not clear to any of them what their next step would or should be.

Chapter 74

The follow up interviews with the staff had begun at Shangrila and one by one each staff member was called to make an appearance at the small café near the swimming pool, with the least likely to have been involved called in first in order to eliminate what Sgt. Reardon and Detective Branch had determined would be the most effective way to proceed.

In doing so, Sgt. Reardon, who had his own ideas about how this should be handled, felt they would then be able to create a more substantive short list of the most likely suspects and could focus more on reviewing their original stories and behavior the night of the murder. Alden Haber was not on the short list and one of the first called in to be shown the spot where the murder took place, while his son, Justin, had been placed on the list of most likely to have possibly been involved.

Still considered to be the most likely suspects, were Ted and a few others in town including Henry Jordan who had been seen at Shangrila by several, and not apparently engaged in any particular work that day. Although having been initially thought as just odd, he had, over time, become largely unnoticed and Sgt. Reardon felt they needed to take a closer look at him. Karl Jenkins had also noticeably been there that day attempting to gain the Manager's attention to discuss his proposal for the Inn's laundry. Detective Branch suggested this could be a ruse and needed a closer look although he had initially stated that he was not someone that needed further scrutiny.

Chapter 75

Alden Haber had intercepted the letters written to Justin from Cecily, one by one in the mailbox, having always been the self-appointed member of the family to collect and first see the mail on a daily basis, and had kept all of them hidden in the back of his bureau drawer once he had opened and read them, seething at what he had learned of his son's actions and Cecily's pregnancy. Raging inside, he had neither confided this to his wife nor as yet confronted Justin who had said nothing about the situation and kept largely to himself in his room when at home. Alden Haber, uncertain of the magnitude of his own temper once unleashed, and where it could lead, had been calculating how to deal with the matter concerning his son.

He had decided on mailing all the letters back to Cecily that he had hidden in his drawer, hoping he would send the message that it was, in fact, Justin returning them, as if to say it was over. He tied them up in a bundle with string and readdressed them to her at her parent's, the Watson's home, unaware that she had in fact just moved, and discreetly dropped them off at the counter of the Laundry/Post Office when no one was nearby to witness him doing so.

Cecily had sensibly remembered to report her new address at the post office which had been duly noted and corrected on the front of the small package found in the out box by Karl Jenkins. Ted had picked it up on his rounds that afternoon and delivered it to Cecily's new address, leaving it at the door to her apartment, assuming the one mailbox to the left served only the adjacent unit.

Chapter 76

Frederik had called and was waiting for Elena as planned at the mall parking lot closest to the door where he had dropped her off and she was glad to see him although he looked somewhat fatigued. It was by then after 7:30 p.m. and they agreed to find a place nearby to stay for the night where they could continue talking now that he had been able to at least encounter Frank Grayson at the bank. He had left, feeling what could have been an explosive situation, had somehow either passed or better yet for the time being, vanished. They talked into the late hours of the morning before going to their rooms to sleep for a few hours before continuing on to Elden the next morning which Frederik seemed both nervous and anxious about doing.

Chapter 77

Arriving at ten-thirty in Elden the following morning, Frederik and Elena stopped first at Dora's Cafe' where they found her still happily attending to her late morning customers, serving her ever popular breakfast specialty, blueberry pancakes. Busy as she was, she saw Elena come in and satisfyingly recognized and greeted her across the room although Frederik who had not only grown taller but was now a grown up young man compared to the thin, shy boy she had known, looked unfamiliar to her and she showed no recognition of him as they quietly slipped into a booth until she could come over to say hello.

There was a young man in the kitchen that they could see from where they were sitting and a girl helping to serve which indicated that Dora had managed adequately over the years and kept her small cheerful business running, her life's work and joy. Dora had grown heavier and made no attempt to hide her greying hair but had the same sweet smile and disposition, and the legendary traces of cat hair on her sweater. When she finally had a free moment, she came to sit down with Elena and Frederik to chat.

She told them that Dr. Gregory had passed away which deeply saddened Elena as she had failed to keep in touch with him during the past few years and not said goodbye to the one person to whom she owed more than anyone.

They had placed an order for coffee and pancakes and were about to dig into them when several people came in speaking noisily and excitedly. They had not been there more than a few moments before everyone had heard the news that Sharon Retton had been found murdered. Speechless and stunned, everyone sat motionless for a moment in hushed silence as she was someone everyone in town had at least either seen, known, knew of, liked, disliked or envied but Sharon's name at some point had been on everyone's lips in town.

Elena looked at Frederik who appeared to look shocked. For all his apparent concern for Frank Grayson, racing to prevent him, if possible, from doing anything foolish, and having just related the long story of his experiences including the situation with Sharon's visits to Victor, this seemed an unbelievable occurrence.

The news of the murder at Shangrila was very much by that time a source of gossip and discussion in Victor as well as all the towns around and now another murder had taken place which would set the region spinning and on edge.

Chapter 78

Sgt. Mathew Reardon had felt no immediate need to mention to Detective Kevin Branch anything about his past relationship with Sharon Retton when he found her on the floor of the apartment and had stifled a deep sigh of sadness not knowing how else to react. Stepping past her body into the small bedroom, he had noted the boxes and suitcases piled against the wall, a bag of groceries on the floor near the refrigerator, still unopened, and wondered how Sharon had come from living at the West end of Elden in one of the most fashionable, upscale homes to this small crowded apartment stuffed with, as yet unopened, luggage, boxes of shoes, clothes and personal belongings.

The apartment was thoroughly dusted for fingerprints and Sgt. Reardon and Detective Branch had found no clues of any substance other than a smudged, unidentifiable fingerprint on the edge of the table.

Cecily had returned in the midst of the confusion, found two police cars in front of her apartment, and had initially not been allowed to enter until they learned that while she had been out, she had given the apartment key to her friend Sharon Retton to bring over some of her things as she needed a place to keep them until she was prepared to move.

Connecting this to the murder at Shangrila did not cross Reardon's mind as Sharon, unlike the unfortunate young Indian girl on vacation, had, he knew, a history of displeased suitors, failed romances, himself included, and could among them have had enemies, despite the presumed unlikeliness that anyone would be wounded enough to murder her. Finding her killer now added to the growing anxiety both Reardon and Branch felt and to Reardon in particular who felt personally driven to find and prosecute whoever was responsible. Having a killer or killers at large in this small town had to be stopped and now the pressure would be relentless for them to produce a suspect and proof of guilt before it could go any further. This discovery was, for Reardon, a moment he would never forget.

Chapter 79

A young couple had purchased Elena and Frederik's parent's property and planned to redo the house, bringing the land back to a working farm and garden. Elena had suggested they stop by to say hello and wish them well and they left Dora's amidst the noisy exchanges and stunned patrons discussing the murder.

They stopped to visit Karl Jenkins at the Laundry & Dry Cleaning establishment and found him chatting passionately with a group of neighbors who had also already heard news of the murder. He was clearly pleased to see Elena and Frederik, having enthusiastically closed the sale of their house not long before and he greeted them warmly. He had grown a bit broader but was colorfully dressed in one of his many bright sweaters and a pair of tweed slacks which had been hemmed to the appropriate length for his short stature. He explained that his proposal was being considered at Shangrila which would allow for him to take over their entire laundry and dry cleaning work, and was clearly excited about the prospect of expanding his business. The murder, gruesome as it was, would provide endless opportunities for gossip in town and they left him returning to the group with whom he had been speaking in order to not miss any details as he waved goodbye.

Chapter 80

Once she had opened the car door and stepped out toward the path leading to the apartment, the killer had wasted no time in alighting from the car to silently follow her around the corner of the building to her doorway, intending to be there before she could enter and relock the door from the inside. She had stooped to pick up a small string-tied package outside on the stoop and had put the key in the lock when quietly behind her the killer appeared and quickly pushed her inside just as she opened the door. The rest was not difficult as she had conveniently draped a thin scarf around her shoulders which was hurriedly yanked off from behind and used in strangling her before letting her drop to the floor. She had not had a chance to turn and see who her attacker was and despite being anxious to get away, her killer impulsively took a moment to knock over a few pieces of furniture in the room, thinking to create the impression of an attempted robbery. Before hurriedly leaving the apartment, feeling it unwise to either empty her bag or take it lest being seen with it, it remained tossed on the floor beside the door, concealing the small package of letters beneath it.

Slipping quietly back into the car and seeing no one on the street it seemed that the timing for all had been fortunate as people had not yet returned to their homes from work at this still early hour and few lights were on in windows or on porches. In the silence the engine was quietly started, the rear view mirror cautiously checked, and seeing no one and careful to not slam the door or turn on lights, the killer drove slowly more than half way down the block almost to the corner before turning on car lights and disappearing in the dark, heading away.

Chapter 81

Justin Haber had taken the car one afternoon and driven to Hemmings as a much needed little getaway. To his surprise, having purposely gone away from Elden, the first person he ran into was Cecily who saw him the minute he pulled into the parking lot of the small coffee shop where she had stopped. Having gone to Hemmings herself to escape the horror of what had happened in her apartment in Elden, unable to return out of fear, shock and disbelief, she had found a furnished room in a family home with a private side entry. She had not mentioned her pregnancy.

That morning Cecily had been able to speak with her sister and her mother, both showing a great deal of sympathy given what they knew she had just gone through. They had told her that they were speaking with her father about his harsh treatment, feeling they could change the tough attitude he had adopted under the circumstances.

On entering the coffee shop, Justin sat near the door, not immediately spotting Cecily and ordered a sandwich and coffee. When she came over and sat opposite him at the table, he sat very still, his heart pounding and looked across at her small, frightened face, still looking sweet and pretty, with her shoulder length blond hair pulled back in a ponytail. An immediate sadness came over him along with a renewed longing for her.

Cecily who had the trauma of the murder in her apartment to contend with along with her pregnancy, could not find words to express her misery but did say she had felt more than dejected at not having had even one response to her many letters. Justin replied that he had received no letters from her and as she had not been in the apartment when the packet of letters had been picked up and brought in by Sharon, had no knowledge that they had, in fact, been returned although not by Justin.

Fully aware at that moment that what she was saying was undoubtedly true, it occurred to Justin that he in fact never picked up the mail at home and that it had been the normal routine for as long as he could remember for his father to always retrieve the mail from their mailbox. He revealed this to Cecily who promptly understood and not only assumed that Justin's father then knew their secret but also believed that Justin had not seen them. They gazed at one another, this being their first conversation since the day when Justin learned of her pregnancy. There was hope in this exchange that both felt and a sense of possibility when Justin asked to see the room that Cecily had found, thinking it was time for him to leave home as well. This was a sensitive and timely meeting for both.

Chapter 82

It was during the second interview for Alden Haber, this time at the scene of the crime, when something was said by the Inn's Manager that revealed what Alden Haber could not believe. While the identity of the victim had still not been revealed nor discussed, he inadvertently mentioned that it had been an out of town hotel guest who had been strangled thereby at that moment making it horrifyingly clear to Alden what a dreadful mistake he had made and that it had not been Cecily whom he had killed. Shaken as he was at this revelation he appeared to remain calm as he stated that he had not been at Shangrila that afternoon but was in fact at home repairing his own sink faucet which he was certain his wife would attest to. Inwardly quivering and feeling unsteady, he was dismissed as they prepared to speak with the next employee. He headed home with tangled, incomprehensible thoughts, anxious to sit down with a stiff drink and consider what he had just learned.

Having earlier contemplated the fact that his actions in killing Cecily could backfire and put Justin in danger of being a suspect once it became clear that the murdered girl was in fact pregnant and had been seeing Justin, he now felt uncanny relief, knowing that either he or his son would be considered far removed from any association with an unknown hotel guest whom neither would have had any reason to murder. Apprehension and dread nevertheless lingered in his mind as he realized that there was still the threatened inconvenience of Cecily and her pregnancy to be dealt with.

The opportunity had been an unexpected one the night he had gone to investigate a small plumbing job near the pool at Shangrila. A water puddle had formed around the outdoor shower faucet when not in use and Alden had remembered it being mentioned to him on an earlier occasion. Thinking of stopping at the inn for a drink that evening just as it had slowly begun to get dark he had first gone by the pool to take a look at the problem when he saw Cecily sitting alone with a book, her head wrapped in a towel and not a soul nearby. Justin had mentioned on more than one occasion that he had been encouraging Cecily to come and swim at the pool and that she often stayed late trying to avoid detection by some of the others or the manager who knew she was not officially allowed to be there.

It happened quickly, a towel on the ground nearby served to do the job as he strangled her without hesitation from behind and then hastily made his retreat. Alden Haber was a strong and powerful man and had no doubt that she was dead as he moved away from the pool area, staying in the shadows and reaching his car in the parking lot without encountering anyone.

This had not been an official workday for him and he had neither punched in at the office nor mentioned to anyone that afternoon that he was going to the Inn for a drink. This was strangely both a transformative yet horrific experience for him as he was aware that his impulsive action had not necessarily solved a problem but may have created a vastly more significant and far-reaching one than he could not at that moment comprehend. Alden Haber headed home to have the very stiff drink he had initially set out to have that evening. It had turned out to be a day unlike any other and one he would never be able to overcome.

Chapter 83

It was dusk. He had been sitting outside in his car a few doors down the street from where he had followed her after spotting her entering a shop in town less than half an hour earlier. She had driven to the duplex apartment where she had pulled up and was sitting in the car possibly looking at her cell phone and about to get out. While Alden Haber had recognized her blond shoulder length hair, he could not identify the car Cecily was driving although he rarely noticed what anyone was driving other than his own car whenever Justin was at the wheel. This had not been very often lately as Justin had spent more and more time at home alone in his room, leaving only to go to work at Shangrila and avoiding conversation at the dinner table. Little had he known at the time that his father knew his secret, had read Cecily's letters addressed to him which he had in fact not seen, and his personal agony in not knowing where he could turn.

Alden Haber had failed once to turn things around for his son and for his family name but now had another opportunity, boldly feeling he was in the clear and confident enough to now take care of what had to be done once and for all. He had made a terrible mistake in attempting to set things right in not realizing who he was attacking at Shangrila, which had left him feeling more annoyed than guilty.

Chapter 84

Sgt. Reardon and Detective Branch, after their initial arrival at the apartment where the murder had taken place, returned and spoke again with Jake, the handyman who had reported the murder. After he had repeatedly stated he could not provide any useful information, they continued their hopefully productive mission of again knocking on neighboring doors in case anyone had been at home and seen or heard anything. Going from house to house on the street, after a few unsuccessful tries, with either no one as yet at home or the few who were, stating they had not seen nor heard anything, they found the answer they were looking for.

The tenant a few houses down on the opposite side of the street who had been walking his dog had stopped by a bamboo thicket no longer confined to the owner's yard but growing out of control onto the sidewalk across from the apartments where the overgrowth had formed a kind of miniature bamboo forest. Quietly waiting for his pet to perform, he had stood motionless amid the bamboo trees and watched someone step from his car, not slamming or even appearing to shut the door, and return hurriedly in what seemed like moments, only to start the car and drive nearly a block in the dark before turning on his car lights and speeding away. His description of the big man he had seen, the color and make of the car, not lost to him although it had been just an idle, curious observation, served to lead them to Alden Haber's residence.

Chapter 85

Simultaneously with the information obtained from the witness, and Sgt. Reardon's and Detective Branch's arrival at Alden Haber's home to arrest him, Justin, after his meeting with Cecily, had comprehended what he was then certain to be the answer to the mystery of the two murders. He realized how in inadvertently killing the wrong girl not once but twice his Father had sought to spare both himself and Justin the ordeal and inconvenience as he saw it of Cecily's pregnancy along with the shame it could bring to all of them including her family, bizarrely imagining her death to be the most effective way to solve the problem.

Justin stepped outside the back door of the house just as the two officers appeared in the yard, having quietly pulled up in front after seeing Alden Faber's car parked in the front driveway. They had knocked on the front door, and when there was no response, had walked separately around to the rear of the house not knowing what to anticipate.

Alden Haber sat motionless in a low patio chair facing away from them directly in front of a large tool shed. Beside him on the ground lay an empty whiskey bottle. When Sgt. Reardon called out to him and there was no response, all three of them walked closer only to discover that he was no longer holding the pistol with which he had shot himself as it had fallen to his lap.

Alden Haber had ended his life once he realized he had mistakenly murdered not one but two, neither of whom were his intended victim, and in so doing, the two tragic murders that had affected the lives of so many others and held Elden hostage had been solved and the terror and hardship of the events concluded.

***

NOTES

o *Cecily and Justin made the coffee shop in Hemmings their good luck haunt and began making plans to be together to begin their family. They felt unclouded for the first time in many months. They were so young.*

o *Karl Jenkins, finding that appointments to make his presentation for the Laundry & Mending Company to take over the business at Shangrila had been continuously interrupted by the murders going on in town, was finally able to gain the attention of the manager and dressed in his best herringbone slacks, orange cable knit sweater and a jacket he had not worn in years which could no longer be buttoned, successfully presented his plan and was awarded the contract. He would now be needing more help to manage the front desk and handle the customers for the Post Office as well and he had his eye on young Justin Haber who was anxious for more permanent work as he was rumored to be getting married and starting a family.*

o *Gloria Retton, with no explanation, had abruptly not returned to her job in Vincent after the shock and disappointment had worn off. Frank Grayson had regained his senses, thrown himself into his work and begun preparations to open another branch of Tecto. He focused more time on his involvements in town and responsibilities on the Boards he was committed to as well as looking forward to planning a long vacation with his wife once the new office was up and running.*

o *Having been aware for some time of her husband's irrational behavior and presumed infidelity, Mrs. Grayson left unexpectedly one morning for the airport and a vacation alone that she had been contemplating and planning for some time.*

o *People in the towns of Elden, Hemmings, Everton, Victor, within the complex of Shangrila and in other communities nearby all thrived on the gossip surrounding the two murders and Alden Haber's suicide. Reluctant to fall back into the routines of small town living without the sudden excitement and mystery that had dropped in unexpectedly on their quiet existence, it took some time before the residents of Elden would allow life to get back to what had been considered normal.*

o *The Chandras and Mr. Sharma decided, after much encouragement from their ever appreciative assembly of customers and passers-by, to remain and carry on what had become not only a successful business due to their sensibly chosen location and hard work but because they had found not just customers, but supportive friends and community* neighbors, whom they felt genuinely cared about them and the predicament in which they had so unfortunately been placed. They would never return to Shangrila.

o Sharon's death had been a huge blow and awakening to Bill and Gloria Retton, and in an unexpected way had served to bring them together. Both at that point recognized how much they had been fortunate to have and yet had not made an effort to enjoy together. They realized that a separation would be more painful than gratifying at this stage in their lives. Deciding to create what would hopefully be a new beginning seemed right. They put their large, and by then unnecessary, home on the market, planning to do some traveling together. Bill could now retire and Gloria was finally able to appreciate all he had done for her. They still found each other attractive and were both prepared for something new. Gloria sold her silvery blue convertible.

o Bill Retton and Frank Grayson never met again.

o Mathew Reardon was also ready for something fresh and new, having from the beginning felt his return to Elden would be only temporary. He had experienced a taste of life in the small corner of the world where he had grown up and later returned, and knew there would be much more waiting for him to see, learn and do.

o His notice was not a surprise to Sheriff Kastor who was reluctant to see him planning to leave but had been proud to see him do the fine job he did. Mathew would be hard to replace. The two murders and the related commotion and uproar had been a troublesome matter. He longed for life to eventually get back to normal in Elden. Detective Branch stayed on for the time being. Henry Jordan and Sheriff Kastor commenced their poker games and left often to go fishing together.

o Just as Elena and Frederik had once been restless and anxious to leave Elden, others had as well, as their lives intermingled and their stories unfolded. They were glad to leave Elden to return home. Frederik earned for himself a handsome position as a Tecto Manager once he graduated. Elena went back to her work with the kids at the camp ready to continue with the programs she had initiated, knowing it was unlikely that Mathew Reardon would be part of her future.

o It had been a noteworthy time.

xxx

Printed in the United States
By Bookmasters